# THE
# IMMORTAL
# GAME

# MIKE MINER

# THE IMMORTAL GAME

www.gutterbooks.com

**The Immortal Game**

Published by Out of the Gutter

ISBN-13: 978-0692257791 (Out of the Gutter)

ISBN-10: 0692257799

Visit **www.gutterbooks.com** for other titles and submission guidelines.

Printed in the USA

*For my father, David Weldon Miner*

# ACKNOWLEDGMENTS

This story had its humble beginnings as a piece of flash in the excellent crime fiction site, Shotgun Honey. Thanks to Kent Gowran for accepting it. Thanks also to Joe Clifford, a fine writer and editor, for his support and friendship in general and specifically for helping this little book see the light of day. And to my wife, Lisa, my only port in the storms, thanks for everything.

*"No price is too great for the scalp of the enemy King."*

—Alexander Koblencs

# THE
# IMMORTAL
# GAME

# 1

*It gets dark fast up here. Cold too. These Vermont mountains murder the weak January sun and leave nothing but gray clouds as witnesses.*

*A triangular house on a steep, wooded hillside. The windows glow. Smoke puffs out of the chimney. Quaint.*

*The figure in the woods is nearly invisible, an inkstain on asphalt. Black coat, hat, boots, the figure, wrapped in midnight-colored shadows, creeps panther-like through the snow. Black gloves assemble a sniper's rifle, slowly; the quiet clicks disappear in the wind. The figure becomes deadly, a killer.*

*A silhouette crosses behind a curtain.*

*Inside, a man walks into the kitchen. He chops vegetables for a salad. He's good with a knife. Since moving here, he's worked as a butcher at the local grocery store.*

*Outside, a car pulls into the driveway. Headlights bring the shadows in the forest to life. All but one.*

*The killer holds the rifle expertly, gingerly, like a parent with a favorite child. It is snowing. Perfect. No footprints.*

*A girl steps out of the car.*

*The man inside finishes his second glass of whiskey, takes a deep breath. He'll tell her tonight. Tell her the man she's seeing is William "Whitey" Scarlotti. Yes, that Whitey. Explain where his dreams come from. His dreams offer no witness protection. No immunity. Each night he drowns in a deep bath of blood.*

*This morning he woke up with his fingers around her throat, his eyes full of a bottomless meanness.*

*"Who are you?" she asked.*

*He had no answer.*

*The door opens. Time for answers.*

*The killer focuses. Patient. If you're going to act like a ninja, think ninja thoughts, the man who taught the killer was fond of saying. The voice in the killer's head is the voice of the man inside. Nothing slows down, but the killer is aware of everything, every snowflake is just where it should be. Even this sudden gust of wind was the killer's idea.*

*There is one window with no curtain. It is a small circle on a high wall. From the woods, Whitey and the girl at the dinner table are perfectly framed.*

*The girl, Karen, takes a sip of wine.*

*He knows it's a mistake. But look at her. Those blue eyes don't know from badness. She is unstained. That smile. He should just walk away. Tell her to get out. Don't come back.*

*"You look like you got something on your mind, Billy."*

*Billy Piccolo. That's who she thinks he is. Who he wants to be. He tries to think of his past life as someone else's. Just nightmares. But his memory's too good.*

*"I'm not who you think I am," he says.*

*Just before the killer feels a rush. Like falling. Nothing but the target. No stopping. A finger caresses the trigger. Squeezes. The crack of the rifle echoes beautifully in these quiet mountains.*

*Whitey will never know if the look of surprise on her face is from what he said or the sensation of a bullet hitting her between the eyes.*

*The killer runs. Rifle over shoulder. Boots chug through the snow. Over the ridge, half a mile away, a black Cadillac with no plates waits.*

*Pistol. Spare clips. Coat. Knife. Whitey is out the door. His heart is like a man about to be buried alive. Pounding to be let out. Listen. Footsteps crunch. Up the hill. He watches, watches for that moving shadow.*

*At the top of the ridge, the killer goes flat. Aims the rifle at the cars in the driveway. Hits two tires on each one.*

*Whitey sees where the shots are fired from and he's off, weaving through trees, fast and quiet. He feels unleashed and dangerous, a drawn sword, and he will not return to his scabbard until he has tasted blood.*

*The killer is tumbling downhill. Breathless. Sees the car.*

*Whitey sees it too. Sees a familiar figure in black glide into it. He shoots, but at this distance....*

*The car roars and skids onto the road.*

*Whitey knows who it is. Taught her everything she knows. He imagines her grinning now, looking in the rearview mirror.*

*His wife always had a killer smile.*

## 2

Dylan Thomas Lonagan should have known.

He knew the well-dressed man was a gangster. Knew he was packing. Could see, in an instant, that the man had the thousand-yard stare, the one we get when we kill someone. Lonny didn't have it yet.

The well-dressed man did. Mixed with a little crazy. Maybe a lot.

As he jogged along the Charles River on a weird and warm January morning, that's what Lonny knew.

He should have known the man was there for him.

But he was thinking about chess. The game he'd lost that morning to Vilma, his old caseworker from the C&S Foundation. C&S: Clean and Sober. Eight years now. They'd kept in touch after Lonny's rehab was over. They played once a week, most weeks. He'd never beaten her. That morning, they had played in the lobby of the Copley Marriott. She had a beautiful board, hand-carved wood, from her home, a village in Guatemala.

She was an aggressive and fearless chess player, loved to exchange pieces. He couldn't remember the last time she had finished a game with her queen. She giggled every time he captured hers, as if he had stepped into a trap. Usually, he had. "You are too protective of your lady." Her accent made her seem thick-tongued. Then she would pin him with her bishops, wreak havoc with her knights. "Check, and her sister, mate, amigo," was how every game ended.

"How is life?" she asked.

He grimaced. Life had become something to endure, to get through. The program helped, this one day at a time stuff suited him. Life, real life, was something he missed. His wife, his son, his badge. All gone, like Job's family. At least Job had faith.

Vilma lowered her gaze, tsked him.

After, Lonny went for a jog down Copley until he hit the Charles, then left.

The well-dressed man made a motion with his hand as Lonny passed him. Lonny was still thinking about the game. I shouldn't have traded rooks, she was baiting me. Then the two other suited gangsters appeared. They blocked Lonny's path, arms up. He had nowhere to go. Adrenaline pulsed through his system.

Behind him, a deep, low voice said, "Easy, Lonny. The boss just wants to talk to you.

Lonny calculated, escape routes, witnesses, came up with zero.

"If we wanted you hurt, you'd be hurt."

True enough.

Lonny's sweat turned icy now that he'd stopped running. He shivered, but relaxed his fists, nodded to the first man.

The well-dressed man exhaled, nodded back. He motioned for Lonny to follow him. Lonny and the three gangsters made their way to a black Mercedes sedan. The engine was still running. Who would steal it? Lonny sat in the back with the well-dressed man. Both Lonny and the man were tall but their legs had plenty of room.

"Back to the ranch, Marco," the first man said.

Marco nodded his boulder-shaped head. He was short but powerfully built. His neck was the size of a tree trunk. The two men in front talked to each other in Italian and Lonny realized they were probably brothers. Marco and Polo he decided to call them. They pulled onto Storrow Drive, headed north. The North End. Naturally.

"What's this about?"

"The boss would prefer to tell you."

"Who's the boss?"

The well-dressed man grinned slightly. "Richard Scarlotti."

The mention of the name seemed to make the car ride lower. Richard "Red" Scarlotti was a serious name. Outside of Providence, he was The Boss.

"What does he want with me?"

No one offered an answer.

## 3

In another life, Dylan Lonagan had had one prior involvement with the Scarlotti family. A strange encounter.

In this previous life, Lonny was known as Detective Lonagan. He worked Special Crimes. His job was to find kids or people who hurt kids. He was ruthless, as ruthless as the criminals he hunted, maybe more. Did what he had to do. Which is why he broke every finger of a man's left hand trying to locate a missing eight-year-old boy, a schoolmate of his son's. Which is why, when that yielded nothing, Lonny started on the other hand, using a hammer. Before he broke the man's second pinky finger, the man gave him the child's whereabouts.

The boy was saved. The man was freed and received a handsome settlement. Lonny was fired.

He could have lived with it. The papers branded him a hero. Work was easy enough to find. Boston still had children to find and people willing to pay him for his efforts.

But he couldn't find his own son after he went missing. Never came home from school. Lonny searched every square inch of his son's walk home, of the school, then slowly expanded his search area. Nothing.

Until too late. An anonymous phone call revealed the location of the body.

The sight of his son in a small coffin broke Lonny, cracked him in half. The man with the broken fingers sent the

Lonagans a beautiful floral arrangement and a tasteful condolence card.

So Lonny went to see Whitey Scarlotti.

Red and Whitey Scarlotti had inherited their father's rackets: the women, the protection routes, the dealers, the whole nine yards. Educated in Cambridge at Harvard, Richard was the brains; educated in the back alleys and pool halls of Boston, William the muscle.

He held an audience with Whitey in his kitchen, with his wife, Katherine.

"Call me Kat," she said when she introduced herself. Her nickname on the streets was "Katwoman." Rumor was she had done more hits than Whitey himself.

Lonny had a piece of paper with a name and address.

Whitey smiled. "This would be the guy with the bad fingers?"

Kat snatched the paper, looking like a child at Christmas. "Ooh, goody. It's even better when they deserve it."

Whitey looked at her like an indulgent parent, then back at Lonny. "Can I give you some free advice, Detective?"

"Dylan."

"Don't do this, Dylan. You haven't gone over to the other side yet. You're still with the angels. Stay there, man."

Lonny took out an envelope with cash in it. Put it on the table and stood.

Kat chuckled. "I knew you had it in you, Dylan."

Lonny shook her hand. "A pleasure, Kat. William, thanks for helping me out."

Whitey shook his head and squinted up at Lonny. He had a killer's eyes, but there was an intelligence there that surprised Lonny. He picked up the envelope. "We'll get word to you next week. Take your wife to a show."

"Raul Julia's playing the man of La Mancha at the Colonial," Kat said.

"We need you to go somewhere public, and be seen."

Lonny nodded.

That was probably what did it, Lonny thought. Taking her to a show on top of everything else. Maggie had been so happy to go, such an out of the ordinary thing to do. Just what she needed, she said. Then the police had questioned them. Gently. Not wanting to connect what everyone knew was connected. What Maggie had known was connected.

"You have shamed me, and you have shamed the memory of your son," he remembered her saying. She talked like that, when she got mad. "You have become a criminal. You are damned."

And she left.

He was only half surprised when, a few days later, the envelope with the cash in it was returned to him, in the mail, not a dollar lighter.


Now he was in another Scarlotti home, this one much grander, a few blocks from Hanover. A brownstone that featured, Lonny felt certain, a view of the harbor from the top floor.

He was escorted to an office. Hardwood floors and leather chairs, everything the color of rich chocolate. Red Scarlotti sat behind an oak desk stood.

He shook hands with Lonny. "I believe you knew my brother, William."

# 4

"He spoke very highly of you," Red said, "and suggested if I were ever in a jam that perhaps I could rely on you."

Red sounded like a lawyer, with his well-heeled, stiff-jawed Cambridge accent, and according to the diploma on the wall behind him, he did have a law degree.

"You *are* Dylan Lonagan? Formerly a detective for the Boston Police Department. Fired for—"

"You got the right guy, Mr. Scarlotti."

Red bristled at being interrupted, but restrained himself. "Who's missing?"

Red nodded, closed his eyes. "My son."

"How old?"

"Eight."

"How long?"

"Two days ago."

"Police?"

Red shook his head. He held up a finger. "I think you might understand my lack of faith in the police." He held up another finger. "And for many reasons, I can't have this information made available to certain parties."

Lonny shrugged, not really surprised. "What about him?" Lonny motioned to the well-dressed man.

"To find my son, Mr. Lonagan, I need the best available. You are uniquely qualified. You can interface with the Boston PD but not be encumbered by their rules."

Lonny looked at a picture of Red's son on the desk. For just a moment, Lonny's head swooned with memories of his own boy.

"I assure you, it will be worth your while if you find my son."

Lonny made a dismissive gesture. This wasn't about the money. It was about getting the child back.

"Tell me everything you know, Mr. Scarlotti."

Red nodded at the well-dressed man, who sighed and reluctantly left the room. After the door shut, Red opened a drawer and retrieved a plastic bag with an envelope inside.

"What's this?"

"It arrived this morning. In my mail."

Lonny examined the letter through the bag. "No postage?"

Red shook his head.

"What's it have to do with your son?"

"I don't know. Maybe nothing."

Lonny pulled out a pair of gloves. He opened the bag and extracted a news clipping from the envelope. He couldn't tell what paper the article was from.

> LUDLOW – Townsfolk here are reeling from a bizarre shooting. Katelyn Clancy (25) of Plymouth was found murdered at the home of local butcher, William Piccolo (37). She was fatally shot in the head. Mr. Piccolo is being sought for questioning regarding the crime. Police have been unable to locate Piccolo, who moved to Ludlow six years ago and was employed at Singleton's Grocery as a butcher. The two were reportedly romantically involved. Piccolo is not a suspect at this time.

Lonny turned the article over and saw an ad for bras at Sears.

"What's this mean to you, Mr. Scarlotti?"

"Nothing."

"Nothing?"

Red shook his head.

"Ever receive anything like this before?"

Red shrugged. "Not exactly. I've gotten threats through the mail before. I'm not sure if that's what this is."

Lonny had a sudden thought. "What are you going to do to the people that took your son?"

"I'm going to make sure they never do it again. Is that a problem for you?"

Lonny grinned. "Not really. It might explain you keeping the police out of this. We need to get this clipping and envelope to a lab."

"It's your investigation."

"Mr. Scarlotti, if you hold back on me, it will jeopardize this investigation, *my* investigation. I am interested in one thing: finding your son. I am interested in nothing else. Not you, not your wife, not your business, not how much you pay me."

"Then our priorities are aligned."

Lonny cleared his throat. "Two days ago this happened?"

"My son left for school in the morning. He did not make it there."

"He walks?"

"Five blocks."

"St. Mary's?"

Red nodded.

"He walks alone?"

"Normally with a friend. Danny Meiser. He stops at his house. Danny was sick that day."

"He stopped there that morning?"

"Yes."

"When did you realize he was missing?"

"The school called around ten to say he was absent."

"Does he skip school ever?"

"Not to my knowledge."

"Where is your wife?"

Red took a breath. "Returning from Florida. Landing within the hour."

"She know?"

Red nodded.

Lonny watched him. "When did you tell her?"

Red bit his lip, pulled at his collar. "This morning."

"She in Florida when this happened?"

"Yes."

"Okay. I'll still need to talk with her."

"Of course."

"I assume you've been looking on your own? Are you still looking?"

"Yes."

"You've got more resources than the average man. Who is running that? Your man who brought me here?"

"Vincent. Yes."

"I'll need to hear what he's found out, where your people have looked, who they've talked to."

"Okay."

"I'm going to walk your son's path to school. Then I'm going to get this to a lab. Then I may go to Ludlow."

"You think they're related?"

"A strange coincidence if they're not. I'd like to talk to your wife tomorrow morning. Here's my card. Call with anything."

Red tried to speak but had to clear his throat. "Should we be concerned that there is no ransom note?"

"Yes. But be ready for one. And if it comes, be very concerned."

As he stood, Lonny noticed a chess set in the corner. It was in mid game. "Are you black or white?"

"Black," Red said. "In both games."

Lonny saw another board on the other side of Red's desk.

"Vincent has your retainer. If it isn't sufficient...."

"It will be." Lonny was studying both boards. "You've lost your queen in this game."

"We'll see if it works."

## 5

Christopher was pretty sure he had the board set up exactly like the board in his father's office. Why had his father let him take his queen? A trap. Had to be.

He stood and walked around the table, looking for the danger. Was it too late? He didn't see an immediate threat but that wasn't his dad's style. He tried to see two or three moves down the road. That was the trick, his father was fond of saying. Don't know the next move, know the next ten moves.

Christopher sighed and closed his eyes, the chess pieces still in his brain. He stretched and looked around the room. It wasn't so bad. He remembered the last few times this had happened. He understood that sometimes his father was in danger, which meant that Christopher might be in danger too.

"A bad person might hurt me?" he had asked his father.

"I will never let anyone hurt you." His father pointed to the chessboard. "See the soldiers in the front row?"

He nodded.

"They are protecting the pieces in back."

"Like Uncle Whitey and Aunt Kat?"

"They are like our bishops and our knights."

Danger was just a fact of life in the Scarlotti family. His mother didn't like it. Christopher could tell. Christopher felt a little less safe now that his Uncle Whitey was dead. But he knew, in the way children know things without fully understanding them, that his father was now the most dangerous man in Boston. Of course it helped that his Aunt Kat was the most dangerous person in Boston.

And she was looking after him.

Christopher thought he might see his father's plan. The king. It was easy to forget how dangerous the king could be, even when cornered.

## 6

Whitey had a lot of questions buzzing in his head. One loomed larger than the others.

Were his wife's actions business or personal?

He wasn't sure which was worse. He could understand personal. Could maybe even forgive it. If someone had hired her, who? Not many candidates.

Had she hit the right target?

From where she'd fired, she could have been aiming at either of them. A game of inches. It would have been a tough shot. But if she wanted the girl, why let her go in the house?

To send a message.

So even if it was business, it was personal.

Whitey met his wife in church. Hard to believe now. Saint Leonard's on Hanover. He almost always attended the 8:30 mass on Sundays. Mostly Whitey and a bunch of gray-haired women, a few families, a few old gangsters trying to save their souls.

Whitey knew his soul was a lost cause, but wasn't Jesus a lost cause? He liked the idea of church, of prayer, of salvation. He would sometimes imagine himself as the good thief.

Kat, just a nameless stranger, came slightly late that morning, just after the procession. She sat at the opposite end of Whitey's pew, towards the back of the church. Dressed simply, she wore a black skirt down to her knees, a short sleeved blue sweater. Her skin was olive, her limbs slender and lithe. At the sign of peace, they met halfway in the pew, the church a whisper of blessings.

Brown eyes, high cheeks, a smile that belonged in an old black and white movie. "Peace be with you," she said, offering a warm hand.

Disarmed, he could only stammer, "Peace."

Whitey's prayers turned from his soul to the chance that the woman might return next Sunday.

Whitey did not take communion. Neither did she.

After mass, she gave him a tiny nod and a flash of teeth before genuflecting on her way out.

She was there again the next week. In the same pew when Whitey arrived and sat in his same spot.

Pants this time, and a blue oxford shirt. Her dark hair up and curled. Her exposed neck, for some reason, fascinated him.

He knelt. Whitey's prayers were informal, more like a conversation, in which God of course knew Whitey's thoughts, his sins, his desires. Whitey was grateful. He sat back and chanced a look at her. She returned a smile, mouthed, "Hello."

He felt like he was in fourth grade again, making eyes at Kelly Toomey, whose father would later forbid her from talking to Whitey.

When they exchanged the sign of peace this time, she pressed his hand a bit harder, maybe lingered a moment. Her voice was deeper than he remembered, kind of smoky.

On the way out, he got stuck talking to Father Silva and lost sight of her. It was raining outside. Whitey pulled up the collar of his trenchcoat as he walked through the sanctuary. A black umbrella blocked his way.

She tilted it back, smiling. "Where you headed?"

"Thought I'd get a coffee at Maria's."

"Want to share an umbrella?"

"Sure."

She lifted the umbrella over his head and stepped next to him, their shoulders touching.

"Here," he took the handle from her and held it over both of them.

She put her arm around him as they walked the stone path between the statues of saints. She giggled. He smiled. He did not recognize her scent. The women he knew didn't wear it. She smelled faintly of roses and baby powder.

It was only a few blocks to Maria's Bakery. Whitey went there every Sunday. They sat at a little table near the front window and ordered coffee: espresso for him, cappuccino for her. The smell of brewing coffee and flour and sugar mixed with the rain and the new smell of this girl. Whitey closed his eyes for a moment picking the details out of the air. Then he watched the way she drank.

Something jumpy in her eyes. Was she nervous? Did she know who he was? He sighed. Maybe this is what it was like for regular folks. The nine-to-five crowd, the shop owners, the salt of the earth. What might have been, he thought. He decided to savor this innocence for as long as he could.

"My name's Katherine," she said and there was a sudden hardness in her expression, an unexpected sharp edge.

"I'm William."

She nodded. "I know." She said it like she knew more than his name, like she knew the combinations to every hidden vault in his head. "You're Whitey Scarlotti."

He couldn't speak. He watched, fascinated, as her eyes turned to thin slits and a beautiful cruelty bloomed on her face.

"You hear a lot of things about Whitey Scarlotti in the North End." Her voice was a seductive whisper. "I hear you knew my father, John Sarno."

He did. It took everything he had to keep his expression frozen.

She flashed that killer smile of hers, showed her saber teeth. She leaned forward. "I heard you killed him," she purred, her voice, a secret whispered in his ear.

He stood on shaky legs, certain that she was here to murder him. Sure that she would pull a tiny gun, something dainty and deadly, out of her purse. Whitey knew how to spot an assassin. He spotted one every time he looked in the mirror.

He threw some money on the table.

Katherine chuckled. She could do more damage with her eyes than most people could do with a knife. "Whitey Scarlotti, you look like you've seen a ghost."

She was still laughing when he opened the door and walked outside. Her laughter mixed with the noises in his head: the screams of her father; it had taken a long time, a lot of tears, a lot of begging. "I have a daughter," Whitey remembered him saying. "Don't do this to her." Whitey believed those were his last words.


"Who's the girl?" his brother, Red, asked him later in the week.

They were in their father's house, in his study, sitting across from each other, a chess game between them.

"What girl?" Whitey said, studying the board, looking for a point of attack.

Red chuckled. "This is a small neighborhood, bro. You think those old ladies you go to mass with aren't all yapping about seeing you with the same girl two weeks in a row?"

Whitey exhaled and took Red's rook with his bishop.

"Hey, I don't care, man," Red said. "You don't want to talk about it, we can talk about something else, like watch yourself." Red picked up his knight and scanned the board, calculating, always calculating with that big brain of his. "Checkmate."

"Dammit."

"We're in a territory dispute with the Denatales. Maybe it's not the best time for distractions."

Whitey was still looking at the board. Wondering where he went wrong.

"You're too aggressive. You can't play offense all the time."

"Look, she's nobody. There's nothing to talk about."

Red squinted at his brother, cocked his head. The same look his father used on people he didn't believe. "I hope so, brother. Another game?"

"Fuck off."

The dainty steps of Red's wife walking into the room. Whitey smelled her familiar perfume. He avoided looking at her eyes, like you avoid looking at the sun.

"William Scarlotti, what's this I hear? You got yourself a girl?"

This is what I get for going to church, he thought, and knew his face was turning scarlet.

She came to church the next week.

He was kneeling, and maybe sneaking a few glances toward the back. Out of the corner of his eye he sensed her, same pew, same spot, she crossed herself and knelt.

He fought the powerful urge to look at her, knew all the old ladies were watching, Mrs. Aiello, Mrs. Londino, old Mama Saienni, just praying for some gossip. When he did finally risk a glance, Katherine caught him, and winked at him.

He shook his head, gritted his teeth. What was with this broad?

He wasn't going to offer her the sign of peace, would just stay where he was. But she walked all the way across the pew, grinning the whole time. What was he supposed to do? They shook. "Peace be with you, William," she said. Her eyebrow arched. A question? A taunt? He smiled tightly. He had to admit, he enjoyed watching her walk back to the other side. When he turned toward the altar, all the old ladies were beaming at them.

Whitey looked up at the fans on the ceiling.

When the mass was over, Katherine left in a hurry.

Whitey was relieved, but curious. What gives?

He was distracted on the way to Maria's. Didn't notice the shadows following him, the shadows in dark suits, packing heat, clocking Whitey's movements.

She found him at his usual table. His usual double espresso in front of him. When she sat across from him, Whitey couldn't help but notice the shit-eating grins on the girls behind the counter.

He looked up at her. Hers was a hard face to read. A good poker player, no doubt.

"Did he suffer?"

Whitey took a sip of espresso, put down the cup, trying his best not to look rattled. He adopted the manner he used in police interrogation rooms. He had plenty of experience. "You got the wrong guy."

"Maybe. Maybe not."

Maria placed a cappuccino in front of Katherine and a plate of biscotti. Nobody had ordered anything. "Eat," she said. "Both too skinny."

After Maria walked away, he said, "I don't know what game you think you're playing...."

"No game." She tasted her drink. Rubbed a spot of foam from her nose. "I just hope he did suffer. He was a son of a bitch. And he had it coming."

She dunked a biscotti. Took a bite. Looked at Whitey.

"You are too skinny," he said.

Her eyes widened.

"You know Felicia's down the street?"

"Everybody knows Felicia's."

"Maybe I buy you a meal."

"When?"

"Tonight. Eight?"

"Maybe I'll be there," she said.

He was too busy watching her leave to notice the wise guy across the street taking notes with his eyes.

Felicia's was on Hanover, up a flight of stairs. You walked past pictures of celebrities eating there. Sinatra, Bob Hope, Roger Clemens.

She kept him waiting a half hour.

They started with red wine and clams casino.

She grew up in Brighton, went to college at Suffolk. Her mom passed away two years ago. Cancer.

"Tough break," Whitey said.

"That's the way the cookie crumbles," she said. Her eyes were not looking for sympathy.

"Tough not having family around."

She shrugged. "I wouldn't know."

He wanted to apologize. Almost said the words.

She shook her head. "No apologies, Whitey. I don't want to talk about it."

"What do you want to do?"

"I want to get out of here."

*

He was nervous. Self-conscious. He wanted to impress her. Hadn't felt that way in a long time. He didn't say much when they got to his place, as she explored his Spartan apartment. He watched her drag her finger along his leather couch, inspect the few pictures on the walls, mostly black and whites of his family. She asked who they were and he told her the truth. She nodded.

"Nice," she finally said. "Simple."

"I bought it for the view," he said and opened the curtains to reveal Boston Harbor.

"That's worth the price of admission."

Watching her, framed by the scene and reflected in it, his breath caught, he would always look back at that as the moment he fell for her.

"Come here," she said.

She tasted like the good red wine they had with dinner; he nibbled her earlobes and was rewarded with groans. She pushed him against the glass door and pressed into him, her breath rushing against his face, his neck, her hands feeling down his chest, his stomach, tugging his belt.

They started on the couch, their pale reflections danced and writhed among the boat lights in the glass.

Her body was like a gift he was unworthy of but still greedily devoured; she was wiry and supple and demanding. Eventually they made it to the bedroom and got down to serious business. She kept asking for more. He provided it.

To break into an apartment with a good security system is not rocket science. All one requires is money and an inside man to pay off.

In Whitey's apartment building, that man was Hassan, known as Hoss by most of the tenants. Whitey knew the secret to breaking and entering, and he knew Hoss would be approached some day by hard men offering hard cash. Hoss had strict instructions of what to do. Hold out for as much money as possible, then provide them access. All Hoss had to do was give Whitey the signal. Let his home phone ring three times, wait thirty seconds, then let it ring once more. The rest was up to Whitey.

His home phone had never rung before that night. Whitey paused.

"If you answer that phone...."

It was the signal. Whitey shifted her toward the nightstand, where he kept his .38 with the silencer.

Two of them. The two that had been tailing him all day. They used the key Hoss had provided. Guns drawn, they slunk into Whitey's apartment. He was still with the woman. Excellent. She was not quiet. Silently, the two men shared lascivious grins. One pointed toward the noise. The other man nodded and they tiptoed single file down the hall.

The bedroom door was shut. Damn.

But Whitey clearly had his hands full. The first man held up three fingers. Then two. One.

Whitey's hands were full. He caught the first man between the eyes, the second in the chest, like target practice.

Kat's head hung off the bed upside down, her hair brushing the floor. She looked back up at Whitey, who made to separate from her. She squeezed her legs around him.

"Don't go without finishing."

Whitey let his pistol fall to the floor. He knew at that moment, that this girl was trouble. He couldn't have cared less.

# 7

Lonny arranged for his Uncle Tom to set up a meeting with the Chief of Police of Ludlow, Vermont, Herb Eddie.

Ludlow, at the base of Mount Okemo, had prospered from the ski boom, and this time of year out-of-state plates outnumbered local ones. Lonny's grandmother had been born and raised there with his uncles, Tom and Jack.

Chief Eddie had a house on Lake Rescue, right next to his Uncle's spread. Lonny had known Herb since he was about two years old.

"Christ, Dylan Lonagan, nice as hell to see you."

They shook hands. Herb's office was small and messy but charming, just like the chief.

"Tom said you might stop by. What's up?"

Lonny couldn't help but smile. "Well, Chief—"

"Son, you call me Herb, dammit."

"Well, Herb, it's about that mess you had a few days ago."

Herb nodded. "Uh-huh. I kinda figured. Mind shutting the door, partner?"

Lonny pulled it shut.

Herb rubbed a hand down his face. "Biggest thing to happen in this little town since who knows when."

"How goes the investigation?"

Herb gave a weak laugh. "What investigation?"

Lonny raised his eyebrows.

"Fucking men in black took it over."

"The Feds?"

"Fucking A. Got a visit from some dude. You know the drill. Clean cut kid, polite, black suit, black tie. Says, Chief, we're taking it from here."

"No shit?"

"I got the victim's family all over my ass, and I don't blame 'em for a second. Christ, it's basically a pig fuck."

"What about this Billy character?"

"The butcher? Between you and me, I doubt it, buddy. They were nuts about each other."

"Did you know him?"

"Sure. Nice enough, for a flatlander."

"He wasn't from Vermont?"

"Nah. Somewhere in Massachusetts, my guess. Had the accent."

Lonny nodded, tried to process all the information. "So they shut you down?"

"In a nutshell."

"You find anything out before they showed up?"

Herb made some noises with his lips as he thought. "Footprints."

"Footprints?"

Herb sighed. "Dylan, what's your interest here?"

"I don't know yet. Might be a link to my client."

"Who's that?"

Lonny shook his head slowly.

"Don't want to share info with your ol' buddy, Herb?"

"You're better off, Herb. And those are the rules. What about footprints?"

Herb narrowed his eyes at Lonny. "Too small. Looks like a sniper job. Professional hit. Through a window from the woods. It snowed on top of the trail so it's hard to tell but I haven't seen feet that small on a killer since the tunnels in 'Nam.

Lonny knew Herb had been in Vietnam. His father and Herb used to stay up late, drinking Canadian beer and comparing war stories.

"Your dad wouldn't have see them. He did most of his fighting in the air."

Lonny's father had been in the First Cavalry. Lonny pictured Herb, tiny but strong, underground.

"In the tunnels, you'd see these little size six footprints. At first I thought they were kid's feet, maybe a woman's."

A woman's, Lonny thought.

"Can I get a look in that house, Herb?"

Herb gave Lonny a shake of his head as he reached into a drawer. "Official Federal Investigation now, Dylan." Herb pulled a key out. "That's a closed crime scene." Herb threw the key to Lonny. "Remember to lock up."

The taped silhouette of the girl was still on the floor, next to the dining room table. A lot of dried blood. Lonny saw the broken window where the bullet had come through. A tough shot.

The décor was pretty simple. A few books, Michael Connelly and James Lee Burke. Nothing very distinguishing. Lonny would have bet the pictures came with the place, all local scenes.

In one of the bedrooms, there was a chess set up, mid game. The black queen was missing. Identical to one of the games in Red Scarlotti's office.

A black GMC Yukon flashed its lights behind Lonny when he got back into town. His head was spinning so rapidly, he wasn't sure how long the car had been in his rearview mirror. He pulled to the shoulder and watched the man in the dark suit and coat hop out and stride to his car. He went to the passenger side, opened the door and hopped in.

He had the usual look. Just as Herb had described him. Short hair, lean face. Lonny figured him for early thirties. Just the start of the sad cynicism in his eyes, which would only grow if he stayed at this much longer.

"Agent Riley," he said, offering a hand. He had a firm grip.

"Dylan Lonagan."

Agent Riley nodded. No doubt, he'd already run Lonny's plates. "What's a PI from Boston doing so far from home?"

"I've got family up here."

"What were you up to in that house?"

Lonny shrugged his shoulders.

"You weren't there long. Find what you were looking for?"

"Just who lived there."

"I could have told you that. Billy Piccolo."

"I bet he looks a lot like Whitey Scarlotti."

"Could be. What's your interest?"

"Not sure yet."

"I've got enough to bring you in if you don't give me something. Tampering with a federal crime scene."

"I think there's a connection to my client. I'm just not sure what."

Agent Riley took out a card, handed it to Lonny. "Look, we've invested countless hours in this guy, in this case. He can put a lot of bad men away. You still remember what it was like? Putting bad men away?"

Lonny remembered.

"You find him, you call me. You get in over your head, you call me. I'd threaten you if I thought it would do any good, but if you get in my way, it will be unpleasant for you."

"Why'd he go G?"

"Scarlotti?"

"Did he go to you or you go to him?"

Agent Riley thought. "He came to us."

"Why?"

"I always figured he was in somebody's crosshairs."

Lonny was having trouble imagining Whitey Scarlotti running from any man. Hard to picture him scared.

"Did you know him?"

"A bit."

Agent Riley nodded. "For a cold-blooded killer, he was all right. Seemed like he was genuinely trying to leave it behind him."

"And now they found him?"

"The bigger question is: will he find them?" Agent Riley opened his door, pulled his coat tighter around his neck. "You get something, call me."

Lonny stayed there, his car on the shoulder of the road until after the agent left, trying to do the math. Too many unknowns. One thing he did know. Based on that chess game, Red Scarlotti had known where his brother was, or at least that he wasn't dead. That deserved a conversation.

# 8

It had made national news, when Whitey Scarlotti had been gunned down while eating at Ida's Restaurant in the North End of Boston.

He had been having a plate of their famous veal and eggplant parmigiana (now dubbed the Scarlotti parmigiana) when three men had breezed in and opened fire. The triggermen were never identified, though everyone assumed they worked for the Denatale crime family.

Except that the execution had been staged by the Feds.

One good thing came out of it. The lines outside of Ida's, always long, doubled. People waited even longer to sit at the table where Whitey Scarlotti ate his last meal.

Now Lonny was back in Red Scarlotti's office.

"When's the last time you heard from your brother, Mr. Scarlotti?"

"William? He's dead. I'm sure you heard about it."

"I sent flowers to the funeral home. But apparently he's turned into Lazarus."

Red let out a breath. "He's still alive?"

"Mr. Scarlotti, do you want him dead?"

Red grinned. Then laughed. "I can assure you, Mr. Lonagan, I'm one of the few people who doesn't want him dead."

"Well somebody does."

"That's nothing new."

"All I care about is finding your son. Why are you sending me to Vermont after wild geese?"

"What if he thinks I sent someone up there?"

"You think your brother has your son?"

"I don't know. That's why you're here."

"When you hold information back, it wastes time. I know trust is not how you got where you are, but if you want your son back, you are going to have to trust me."

High-heeled footsteps in the hallway echoed outside the door.

"Your wife is back?"

Red nodded.

"How's she taking it?"

Red shook his head. The office door opened.

Mrs. Scarlotti was not what Lonny was expecting. Tall and slender, with strawberry blonde hair, pale, freckled skin still red from her trip to Florida, and eyes as green as the emerald isle. Her sweater was green cashmere and her khaki slacks billowed around her skinny legs as she marched into the office in brown leather boots. A stunner, that's what Lonny's father would have called her.

He'd been expecting big, dark hair, flashy jewelry, loud clothes. Not Newbury Street boutique.

Her jaw was stiff, her eyes flashed, first at Red, then at Lonny.

"Any good news to report?" Her voice was quiet. A slight Mass accent just hinted at the second "r" in report. "Has my gangster husband heard from the gangsters who've taken our son?"

She was trying to be tough, cruel, but the tears that ran down her face told another story.

Red and Lonny watched.

She hugged herself. "Where's my boy?" she said to nobody in particular.

"I wish I knew, Mrs. Scarlotti." And Lonny did, very badly. He would have liked to see this beautiful woman happy. These Scarlotti men, Lonny thought, certainly can pick their women. "What makes you say, gangsters?"

"What?" she said.

"You said gangsters who've taken your son. What gangsters?"

She seemed to regard Lonny closer now. "I guess I just assumed that it was . . . family business."

Family business.

"What do you think?" she asked him.

"I don't know yet." Lonny did not see a reason to educate the Scarlottis about the monsters who prowl the world for young boys.

"If it were gangsters," Lonny asked, "who would it be?"

Red said nothing.

"The Denatales," Mrs. Scarlotti said.

Lonny knew the history, the feud.

Red nodded.

"Anyone else? Anyone new in the area, looking to make a splash? Any old vendettas?"

"The Denatales would have the most hard feelings," Red said. "Lately, since the old man's been in the joint, his son has been running things."

A new player with old grudges. But no word yet. No note. No call. Just letting them stew over it?

Or was it someone else?

# 9

Kat Scarlotti hated waiting. She was a woman of action. Which was why, after Whitey died—or didn't as it turned out—she kept taking contracts. The action. The rush when she turned out somebody's lights.

Ever since that first dead body in Whitey's apartment years ago, she was fascinated.

She remembered looking closely at those bodies. Their hearts like clocks that had stopped working. Messy clocks. She remembered the blood, thicker and darker and brighter than she had pictured—and much more of it.

"Do they always smell like that?"

"Usually," he said.

She would find out later for herself how sometimes they released their bowels, sometimes even ejaculated. She'd find out for herself what a messy business killing was.

"Maybe you should go home," he said.

"I am home," she said.

She helped. Helped spread out the plastic, watched him roll one body onto it, then wrap it up. Same with the other. She acted as a lookout, opened the doors for him as he carried the corpses, one at a time, to his Yukon.

"I'll be back," he said.

"I'll clean up."

She found his cleaning supplies and scrubbed everything down. Whistled while she did it.

When he got back, she was in the shower.

"You okay?" he asked, coming into the bathroom.

"No."

"What's wrong?"

"I'm lonely."

He opened the shower door.

"Come get clean before I get you dirty again."

She enjoyed the slack-jawed look on his face. She had never seen it before, the look of a man realizing: this is the one.

The feel of him in the shower, like slick stone.

Yes, she was the one. Not some doe-eyed, big-boned farm girl from the north country. Opposites attract. Bullshit. That was why that girl was dead. And any other girls he tried out. Maybe he understood that now.

So she was waiting. For him or for them. A lot of people were unhappy with her. This was the calm before the storm.

She heard her nephew walking down the hall. Put her Beretta inside her pants, against the small of her back. Pulled her sweater over it.

"What's up, Aunt Kat? Any word from Mom or Dad?"

She patted him on the head. Normally, she didn't much care for kids, but she was fond of her godson, Christopher. Sweet and quiet, like his dad and his Uncle Whitey. Fair and delicate like his mother. "Nothing yet, kiddo."

He sighed.

"Hang in there," she said.

"What'd you get at the store? Did you get my Frosted Flakes?"

"I got your Frosted Flakes," she said, pulling the box out of the grocery bag.

The phone rang.

Three times.

A pause.

Once more.

The signal.

Kat's Beretta was in her hands. Christopher's eyes went wide.

She smiled at him. "Remember the drill."

Christopher froze.

Kat slapped him. "To the bedroom. Then do just what I told you."

Christopher bolted to the guest bedroom.

It was a well-kept secret that there was not a tenant upstairs. They owned that unit too. For just such an emergency. Christopher went into the closet, climbed the shelves and popped open the hidden trap door.

So it was them, not him. Good. A nice little appetizer for her. She watched the doorknob turn. Slowly. Quietly. The man never knew what hit him.

She guessed there would be two or three. Figured they'd never expect her to come out the front door after them. So that's what she did. Crouched low, she ran and slid on the tile floor, gun ready, as she came out the other side. For a second, they were stunned. Which was all the time she needed. Pop. Pop. The fourth one (Goodness, Angelo, for little old me? she thought) fired and missed, then turned and ran. She clipped his arm as he rounded a corner. It slowed him down enough for her to get close, shoot his left leg.

He went down.

She stepped close, kicked his gun away. Put her face right in front of his. She liked her pretty smile to be the last thing men saw before they died.

His eyes hadn't realized it yet. Hadn't let go of his life.

"Denatale?" she said.

His eyes stopped darting, settled on hers. Saw what was there for him. He nodded.

She nodded back and turned out the lights for him with a headshot.

What a mess.


The boy climbed the fire escape up to the roof. He took in the view. From here he could see the water, the aquarium, Quincy Market. He listened to the sound of Aunt Kat's gun.

All Christopher could think: Wow.

Two more shots.

So they really were after us, Christopher thought, and suddenly he was worried about his parents. Who was looking after them?

Aunt Kat's head appeared at the top of the fire escape. "All clear, kiddo."

Back inside, Aunt Kat threw things into a suitcase. "Two minutes. Pack everything you need." She handed him a duffel bag.

"For how long?"

"I don't know."

"What's going on?"

"The chickens are coming home to roost."

## 10

The old man was not going to be happy.

Twice in one week things got all fucked up.

Don't shoot the messenger, he thought, as he took the drive to Walpole. MCI – Walpole. Massachusetts Correctional Institute. But it wasn't Walpole anymore, not like when he did his time there. The town had raised a stink. Now it was MCI – Cedar Junction. Call it whatever you want, Angelo Denatale, Jr., thought; it was still a dungeon that stole years in exchange for nightmares.

It took about thirty minutes to get there from Boston, depending on when you left.

Angelo Denatale, Sr., "alleged" head of the Denatale crime family, was awaiting trial. He had been denied bail. For two years, he had run things from the inside, talking to his son three times a week, sending messages, reaching people over the twenty-foot high walls, past the barbed wire and electrified fence.

Plotting—always plotting—revenge against the Scarlotti family, and searching for the Feds' mystery star witness, whose grand jury testimony sealed the arrest warrant. Murder, extortion, racketeering, mayhem, the whole nine yards.

Then they found him. Whitey Scarlotti, not so dead after all. Holed up north somewhere in the Green Mountains of Vermont.

But that bitch had fucked everything up, intentionally or not, and now she had to go. Gone. Forever.

\*

Angelo, Sr. knew immediately that it had not gone well. Could tell from the way Junior was sitting that he was frightened of what his father would do. Even through an inch of glass, his son was scared to death of his old man. Senior almost turned and went back to his cell, a private one, where he received private meals, the only real perk available to him. That and the private showers.

"What happened?"

His son shook his head.

"Complete failure?"

A nod.

"Christ." Senior considered punching a hole in the glass.

Junior was braced for just this reaction. He knew his father well.

"Have we taken care of the men who failed us?"

"She did that for us. But Dad, realize that our . . . problem . . . has gone off the grid. Let me push the judge for an earlier trial. Minus you-know-who, they can't convict. They've got nothing. She may have given us just what we needed."

"Angelo, you're a good lawyer but a lousy criminal." He didn't know where he'd gone wrong, why his son lacked his own killer instincts, why he never wanted to confront problems, just avoid them, sidestep them. Senior sighed.

Junior rolled his eyes.

"Get after the judge. Speed things up. Then get a hold of the German."

"The German?"

Senior nodded.

Junior gulped.

*

The German was not actually German; he was Swiss. But he looked German. He spoke German. The German had spent time in Iraq with the French Foreign Legion, and then later in Afghanistan, the Balkans, Africa. After several tours of duty, the German had settled in Rome and found employment with one of the larger crime families in Italy. After a few years, the German had become quite notorious, as well as quite wanted by the Italian authorities.

Angelo Denatale had sponsored his emigration to America, where he housed him in luxury. Denatale kept him available as a last resort, like a nuclear weapon. Because, word on the street was, the German would get the job done, just not always cleanly. When using the German, one had to account for collateral damage. He lacked the finesse of say Whitey and Kat Scarlotti. But Angelo was prepared for collateral damage in this case. After all this was war.

And if there was any Scarlotti man, woman, or child walking the face of the earth when the German was done, Angelo would murder them himself.

"But remember, son. Until one or both of our problems is solved, I'm safer here than out there," Senior cautioned. "Especially from her."

Junior nodded and saw something he had never seen before in his father's eyes: Fear.

## 11

"Tell me about him."

"My son?"

Lonny nodded. They were in some sort of living room. Beautiful hardwood floors, cherry, he guessed, surrounded a burgundy, patterned rug so thick it grabbed at your feet as you walked on it. A leather couch so lush, Lonny never wanted to get out of it.

"He is handsome."

"I can see from the pictures."

She flashed a sad smile. "He's bright."

"Like his parents."

She shrugged. "What is the purpose of this? What do you want to know?"

"I'm not exactly sure. You learn, in this line of work, to find out everything you can. You never know what piece of information will do it. Better to have as much as possible."

A sigh. "I see."

"Mrs. Scarlotti—"

"Linda."

"Linda, does he have any hobbies? Video games?"

Linda thought. "He likes to read."

"What's he read?"

"Fantasy stuff. *Harry Potter. The Hunger Games.*"

Lonny nodded.

"His father used to read the first few *Harry Potters* at bedtime. Christopher got hooked."

It was difficult to picture Red Scarlotti, the famous gangster, reading to his son about Dumbledore. But it made Lonny fonder of the man, he had to admit. The things men will do for their children…. What did Lonny used to read to his son? Ferdinand. Every night. Lonny read it so often, he could almost recite it from memory. Once upon a time, in Spain…

"Mr. Lonagan?"

Lonny snapped to attention. "Sorry."

"You were thinking about your son."

"Yes." She was a woman who would be hard to lie to. Lonny wondered how Red did it.

"I remember reading about it." As she spoke, she wrung her hands. "Then later, something happened to the man you suspected."

"He vanished," Lonny whispered.

"That's right," she said. "I probably shouldn't say this, but I was happy."

"I was too."

"But you aren't anymore?"

Lonny tried to look her in the eyes, but they only reminded him of everything he'd lost. Those green, green eyes were trying to hold on to everything. Lonny knew how hard it was.

"Does your son know about his father?" Lonny asked.

"You mean," Linda grinned, "does Christopher know that his father is a gangster?"

"I guess that's what I mean."

"He knows his dad has a dangerous job. A few years back there was some trouble."

"The North South War?"

Linda nodded. "Christopher went to live with his Uncle Whitey and Aunt Kat."

Lonny's eyes widened.

"Can you think of safer guardians?"

"I guess not."

"Christopher understands that his father has enemies."

"When did you realize who he was?"

"What does this have to do with finding my son?"

"Nothing." He was just curious. How one won the hand of such a lovely creature.

She closed her eyes and let out a long breath.

"We met in college. Richard didn't put on airs back then. He was a terrible flirt."

She seemed guilty, remembering fond things now.

"We went out a few times. A few places in the neighborhood. Everyone knew him. I figured he was just a popular, local kid." She shook her head. "Things were going well. For Valentine's Day, he decides to take me to Providence, to Federal Hill. The best Italian meal you'll ever have, he says."

"Where'd you go?"

"Camille's."

"Pretty good."

"He was right. The food just melted on your tongue. After dinner, we're waiting for the valets to get our car. There's some guy there. Older. All dressed up. A little wobbly from booze. He's mouthing off to the valets. He looks at me, then turns to Richard, says, that is a fine piece of ass."

"The valets go bug-eyed. Richard stays calm and cool, doesn't even raise his voice, just says, "Watch your mouth, sir." Gives him his dead-eyed stare. My jaw drops. The old guy loses it."

Lonny pictures it, this Ivy League, Irish catholic girl, in the middle of all these gangsters.

"Who the hell you think you're talking to, you little punk, the guy says. Richard keeps giving him the eye. The old guy pulls out a gun. The valets wrestle him inside. I'm saying, Richard let's get the hell out of here. Richard doesn't say a word, but his face is bright red and he's shaking. I thought it was fear."

Not fear, Lonny thought. Anger.

"The valets must have explained who Richard was because a few minutes later, out comes the guy, red faced, near tears. I say, Richard let's go, but he keeps looking at the guy. The guy won't make eye contact with anyone but finally he looks at Richard. Richard is twenty years old, mind you. Guy looks straight at Richard, clears his throat, and says, I'm terribly sorry, Mr. Scarlotti. Richard gives him one of those smiles that isn't a smile. Turns to the valets and says, Make sure this guy gets home safe.

"Now, my friends had made some jokes about Richard, some mob jokes. I never took them seriously. When we got back in the car, I turned to him and said, Who are you? He laughed. Just some guy with a mean dad, he said."

"Lorenzo Scarlotti," Lonny said. The boss of bosses.

"A lot of people would have known right then what they were in store for and gotten the hell away from him."

"But not you," he said.

She sighed and looked at him. "Not me." She sniffed. "You think this is all my fault."

"No."

She smiled. It did things to his chest, her smile, made it hurt. Maybe that was just his heart, rusty at beating fast. "You're a lousy liar."

Lonny chuckled. "For what it's worth, Linda, the heart wants what it wants. The choices aren't always easy."

Linda's expression changed. She looked away then back at him. "My husband mentioned…." She turned away again.

"What?"

"His brother, William."

"Yes?" He tried to read her expression, but it was tough. Concern? Fear?

"He's still alive?"

"He seems to be. Have you heard from him?"

She shook her head. "I can't believe it."

Lonny decided to leave it alone. "I'm being paid to find your son. I'll go try to do that."

"Thank you, Mr. Lonagan."

"Dylan."

"Thanks, Dylan." She touched his arm, squeezed it.

It made him want to kill people for her.

# 12

Whitey was in a car across the street.

Lonny walked out of the Scarlotti house.

Whitey watched him. Remembered him. Wondered how much he could trust him.

He remembered the Lonagan job. If you could call a free hit a job. Whitey had been happy to do it, though Kat had pulled the trigger. Whitey had cleaned up. Made the man disappear. He remembered the man's things, his secret stashes of child porn. Whitey shivered at the memory.

"We should let the cops find this stuff," Kat had said.

Whitey shook his head. He didn't want Dylan Lonagan to know about it. Didn't want him tortured by it.

"What if one of these kids is his?"

"Then he's better off not knowing."

Whitey had stuffed all of it, boxes of filth and the man's body, into the back of his Yukon. Took them all out of town and set fire to them.

As he watched the flames build and devour the man and the records of his sins, Whitey wondered what it would be like. To fight crime for a living. Make the streets safer.

Whitey watched Dylan Lonagan and wondered again. What would it be like to be a hero? To get called to save people instead of kill them?

*

His son dead.

His wife gone.

Sooner or later that dark whirlpool sucking at your feet, pulling at your legs, that bitch, despair, wins the battle and pulls you under to a dark world full of shadows and whispers, an inferno where hope is abandoned and everything is your fault.

But this wasn't hell. There were ways to quiet the voices, dim the fingers pointing at you.

Things got pretty bad for Dylan Lonagan.

Boston's an easy town to drink in. Especially when everyone knows your name. Everyone knew his story. Saving the kid, getting kicked off the force, losing his son. It made for entertaining reading; it sold papers, like any story that keeps getting worse.

There were plenty of people to buy him drinks. Plenty of cops to look the other way when he'd had too much.

One night, Whitey saw him stumble past the front window of Modern Pastry. Sometimes, after a job, Whitey liked to sit and unwind with an espresso and a biscotti, liked to act civilized, kid himself that he was.

Lonagan looked a mess, hair wild, eyes squinting. Whitey saw some local boys tailing him. He sighed and stood.

Just past the pastry shop, across the street was St. Mary's Church. In front is a garden, a statue of Mary held center stage. The drunk saw her and wanted to chat.

The three boys saw an easy score. The drunk was on his knees, praying.

"I don't know what to do, Mary. I don't know what to do."

His hand touched her stone feet. He sobbed.

The oldest boy grinned, turned to the youngest boy. "All right, Jimmy, go pop your cherry. Take his wallet."

Jimmy nodded, then looked past the oldest boy, over his shoulder.

The older boys turned.

Every wannabe gangster in the North End knew Whitey Scarlotti. Wanted to be him. They looked in the mirror and practiced his dead stare. The same stare now directed at them.

"Not him, boys. He's with me."

They couldn't leave fast enough.

"Yes, sir, Mr. Scarlotti."

"Just keepin' an eye on him."

Whitey barely acknowledged them. He concentrated on Dylan Lonagan. The life of a hero. Heavy is the head.

Those kids still talk about the night Whitey Scarlotti stopped them from robbing some lush outside of St. Mary's, and how shocked they were later, when they saw Whitey carrying him down the sidewalk over his shoulder. Nobody said a damn word to him.

Whitey followed Lonny, observed him get a phone call and change his destination. He was surprised when Lonny walked past a group of police cars and patrol men, all painted the color of flashing lights, and into Whitey's old apartment building.

Lonny stood in the living room of Whitey and Kat Scarlotti. The room was full of cops. Detectives and forensics.

He remembered waking up there. Years ago. The same couch. His head felt like hammered tin. Dented. He had no idea where he was. The soothing voice of a woman singing. Breakfast smells, the pop and sizzle of something frying in a pan.

"You're up?" Kat Scarlotti said.

"Where am I?"

"It ain't Kansas, Dorothy."

Lonny cradled his head.

"Can you eat?"

"I'm not sure."

"You should." She put a plate in front of him. "You throw it up, I won't take it personal. Coffee?"

"God, yes."

An omelet. Just a bit of cheese, a mix of herbs, tomatoes.

"This is amazing," he told Kat when she brought his coffee in.

She smiled. "We aim to please here at Casa Scarlotti. Grew those tomatoes ourselves, out on the deck.

Lonny sipped his coffee.

"Not bad for a killer, huh?"

"Not bad at all."

They sat for a while. Lonny couldn't remember the last time he'd eaten, let alone something this good. Kat sipped her coffee and seemed quite content to watch Lonny enjoy her cooking. What had happened to her, he wondered, what had broken her, turned her into what she was?

"He suffered." She turned her eyes on him. "If that helps."

He had never seen kindness and wickedness teeter so precariously in one person before.

"I don't know if it does."

She nodded. "I hoped it would. Whitey knew it wouldn't, didn't he?"

"I guess he did."

"That damned conscience of yours."

"I suppose." Maybe that was what she was missing. A conscience. "How'd I get here?"

She giggled. "I'm sorry. Whitey brought you. Carried you more like it."

Lonny grimaced. He had no recollection of it. The last thing he remembered was a man buying him a drink and slapping him on the back. "This is one of the good guys," he'd said. Lonny couldn't down his drink fast enough. He wished he'd drunk enough to forget that line. One of the good guys. Used to be.

"He's worried about you."

"Who?"

"Whitey."

"Where is he?" The whole scene was so incongruous, sitting here, chatting with the infamous Kat woman, like they were old friends.

"Whitey? It's Sunday. He's at church."

"Wouldn't have figured him for the church-going type."

"He never misses."

"A true believer?"

"Yes."

"So...."

"So he knows he's damned."

It was a difficult piece to place in the puzzle of William Scarlotti. Lonny's picture of him kept changing. Did he want to redeem himself?

"Kat, you're a great hostess."

Lonny could almost smell the breakfast Kat had made for him all those years ago. A wistful smile played on his face.

"Who called it in?" Lonny asked the detective, a man named Miller.

"Two calls. Building across the street."

Lonny smiled. "Nobody from the building?"

Miller shook his head, the same smile on his face. "Four dead bodies. She got the last one between the eyes."

Miller was pointing to the corpses splayed on the floor. Typical goons from the looks of them.

"All carrying. Looks like self defense." Miller rubbed his eyes. "Word is, you're working for her brother-in-law."

Lonny nodded.

"Missing kid?"

"Maybe."

"Check out the far bedroom."

Lonny walked down the hall. Stepped into the room.

The unmistakable signs of a young boy. Superhero comic books, Harry Potter DVDs, in the closet, young boy's clothes.

A chess set.

A familiar game.

Lonny looked at Miller and nodded.

"Fingerprints will confirm it."

"I figure," Miller said.

"How long have these stiffs been stiff?"

"Not long. Two hours, tops. They aren't even stiff. Now I got a question for you. Why would Kat Scarlotti have Red's kid? And who were these dudes after? Kat or the boy?"

Lonny shrugged. He had the same questions. He fought the urge, the old reflex, to order the cops in the apartment around. "You recognize these guys?"

They were back in the living room.

Miller crouched close to one of the dead men's faces. "Giuseppe Rossi. Footsoldier for Angelo Denatale."

Curiouser and curiouser.

"Looks like the start of something," Miller said.

Lonny nodded. He thanked Miller. On his way out, he looked at the door, turned back. "How'd they get in?"

Miller shrugged. "No sign of forced entry."

And curiouser.

*

Lonny wanted a drink but settled for a double espresso at Mike's Pastry. No sugar. This time of night there was a decent crowd. Lonny sat at a table and breathed the smell of confections, like the air was part sugar, part butter.

A tall man entered, wearing a leather jacket with chains on it, a blue bandana around his head and a scowl on his face. The sort of man you noticed immediately then looked away from. Unless you were a certain type of woman.

Even Lonny, trained at spotting faces in crowds, didn't make him at first glance. But there was something familiar about him. The dead, dark eyes. The man didn't move like a typical tough guy biker, heavy on his feet. Pulling out a chair at Lonny's table, the man's movements were careful, graceful.

Whitey Scarlotti.

Lonny sipped his espresso, put the cup down. Whitey ordered the same from the young waitress.

"Long time," Lonny said.

Whitey smiled. Raised his eyebrows.

"There's a man in a black suit looking for you in Vermont."

Whitey let out a long breath. "I need to know what happened in there."

"Was it Kat that shot up your place up north? Killed that girl?"

They spoke quietly, leaning toward each other. Whitey's disguise had the effect of making people ignore them. They stopped talking when the waitress put down the tiny espresso cup.

Whitey took a small sip. A look of fond remembrance washed over his face. He took another sip. "Christ, I missed this stuff."

"Was it Kat?"

"Why are the cops in my apartment?"

Lonny held up four fingers. "Four of Denatale's men."

"Kat?"

"She split."

"We need to talk to Hoss."

"I need to talk to your brother. Who's Hoss?"

"The doorman. Hassan."

No forced entry, Lonny remembered.

"Why do you need to talk to Red?"

"Christopher was there. He's been missing."

"My nephew?" Whitey covered his face with a hand. He shook his head slowly back and forth, eyes closed. "That's why you're in on this."

"Yes." Lonny stood.

"Okay, I'll find you later."

"Any message for your brother?"

"I'll deliver it myself."

## 13

The German was watching. His blue eyes clocked every detail of these two men. Perhaps they could lead him to her. The one man was obviously police. Either now or in a past life. Maybe he was private. The other was not what he appeared. The clothes he wore, the bandana, these were affectations. He moved like a soldier, head on a swivel. The German realized he would not be able to follow this man too closely, for if he saw the German's face, he would not forget it.

There was a blankness to this tall man's eyes, a hardness that the German recognized. This man had seen how bad things could be, and so spent most of his time observing the world with dull recognition. Only rarely would those eyes go wide, as they just had, and only when faced with true beauty or true horror.

The man was a killer. It took one to know one.

The policeman left first.

The German decided to stay with the other man. He risked stopping across the street for a moment; the lights in the shop would make looking out through the front window difficult.

The man sipped his coffee. The German watched, jealously, from the cold sidewalk, in a heavy winter coat and wool cap.

Something changed in the tall man's face. A softness crept into his eyes. What? A memory, a regret? What warms your cold heart, he wanted to ask.

But then the man's eyes shifted focus. Looked out the front window.

The German had lingered too long.

The man had registered the still shape in the window. He stood.

The German ran, dashed down an alley, over a fence.

He would have to be careful with this one.

He twisted his route, doubled back, slowed to a walk, got his breathing under control. He stepped onto Prince Street when he heard a heavy step behind him.

"Nice night for a stroll."

The German paused. A smile on his face as he turned slowly toward the voice, the man from the coffee shop. The killer. A deep voice, ragged, and just a bit playful. The man knew what he was playing, who he was playing with. The German could see the tension in him, an echo of his own. Both men poised, ready for a sudden move.

Their eyes met, eyes that had seen a lot of people die in front of them.

"Yes, it is," the German said.

Now is not the time, their eyes said, but both men felt the chilly knowledge that the time would come. Soon.

They both smiled. With anticipation? Curious to find out who the best was, but willing to wait.

# 14

"Let me get this straight," Red Scarlotti said. "There are four dead men in Kat's apartment right now? Denatale's men?"

"Yes, sir."

"That's an act of war."

Red's hands were fists, his eyes and mouth thin slashes on his face.

Linda Scarlotti was pale. Her eyes never left Lonny's face. She knew there was something else. "Dylan, tell us what you came to tell us."

Red's face was a mixture of rage and confusion. "What else?"

Lonny cleared his throat. "There were signs that a young boy had been staying at Kat's."

Linda's hands trembled, her eyes shiny with tears. "Is he OK?"

Lonny held up both hands. "There's nothing to indicate that anything happened to him."

Linda sighed.

"I don't understand," Red said.

"Neither do I," Lonny said. "Neither of you knew about this?"

Both just stared at him.

Lonny's head hurt from the effort of trying to connect these dots. He felt like a man juggling chainsaws, not sure where he needed to grab.

Red looked ready to explode. Lonny thought of Napoleon or Hannibal, a general with his army cornered, trying to decide the proper course of action.

Linda's voice fluttered out of her pretty mouth. "What do we do?"

"We find Kat. We find your son. Mr. Scarlotti, if anything changes, I'll be in touch. Keep me in the loop on your end. And think about this—" Lonny waited for Red to look at him. "You can't go toe to toe until your son is out of the line of fire. The old man knows that. So watch yourself."

Reluctantly, Red nodded.

Linda walked Lonny out. "You don't think Kat would...."

"I don't think Kat would harm a hair on that boy's head."

"But she's a killer, just like her husband."

"Look what she did to the men who threatened your boy."

"I think she's come unhinged."

Lonny thought of the woman who had made him breakfast years ago. Was he letting that small act of kindness cloud his judgment? He had glimpsed a rarely seen side of her.

Linda took Lonny's hand in hers. "Find them. Bring my Christopher back to me."

Lonny nodded, but in his head it was another boy he saw, another woman asking him to do the rescuing.

She seemed to sense his pain. "What was his name?"

Lonny looked at his feet. "Ryan."

She touched his cheek, lifted his face. Her eyes were filled with tenderness. Lonny tried to remember the last time a woman had looked at him like this, touched him like this. His son's face rose up before him instead, and Lonny wondered for the millionth time, what his son's face looked like before he died. Had those innocent, sky blue eyes witnessed how horrible the world could be before they shut forever?

She was saying, *He's upstairs putting a war party together. Be my soldier, my avenging angel. Find him. Save him. Please.*

Her lips on his cheek nearly knocked him over.

The first sip is like a first kiss, tender, tentative, sweet, like falling in love.

The first drink is like popping your cherry, fast and fun and over too quickly, no matter how you try to savor it. Leaves you thirsty for more.

So you have more.

Then the night turns into a child's finger-painting.

It was not exactly like riding a bicycle for Lonny. More like riding a bicycle with no hands. He stumbled from bar to bar, as if riding downhill, pulled by some force, in and out of those seedy dives.

The German observed all of this with curiosity.

Every man has his breaking point. He had seen it many times. Every man handles it differently. The German's impression was that this man had been broken before but he suspected this man might still rise up, might still prove dangerous.

The German did not want to underestimate him.

The bartender would not serve Lonny. Well, he would serve him water.

Lonny could not understand why. "How long have we known each other, Joe?"

The bartender looked at his watch. "Five minutes."

"What are you talking about, Joe?" Lonny spoke as if someone were squeezing his cheeks together. "We go way back."

"My name's not Joe."

"Man, you've changed. You used to have magic in those bottles."

"Let me call you a cab, buddy."

"That's okay." Lonny's shoulders slumped. "I live just around the corner." He held his face in his hands. "The old lady will not be happy with me."

The bartender nodded. "Well, go face the music. The sooner the better."

Lonny nodded. Knocked on the bar. "Thanks, Joe. You still got it." Lonny fell off his barstool.

A blond man with icy blue eyes helped him up.

Kelly knew who it was ringing her buzzer. Knew what condition he would be in. Another buzz. Black out drunk. He'd had a good run lately too. Years. She considered ignoring him, but she had to confess: she did not want to be alone tonight. Even if that meant being with the man who had ruined her life. It was comforting being with someone who understood her pain, who had been burned by the same fire, even if he had lit the match.

"Come up, Lonny." She buzzed him in.

Lonny's feet stumbled and his voice echoed towards her apartment door. "Salt of the earth," he said. "You'll never meet a finer woman."

She rolled her eyes and opened her door.

There was a man with him, basically carrying him up the steps. Lonny's arm was around his neck.

"Honey, sorry I'm late. Traffic was a bear."

All sorts of witty replies came to her but she was reluctant to carve up her ex in front of this stranger, who stopped and, with two hands, held Lonny at the threshold of her apartment. He nodded to her.

He was handsome in a generic, Brooks Brothers model sort of way. "Ma'am," he said quietly as he let Lonny go.

Lonny teetered, as if his feet were trapped in cement. Kelly caught him in one arm, a familiar act.

"Thanks, mister."

He nodded. She didn't like the way his eyes seemed to be everywhere. "He spoke very highly of you."

"I'll bet he did." She backed away. "Thanks for getting him home in one piece."

"My pleasure."

His eyes were like polished steel and his gaze made her shiver. Those eyes stayed on her until she shut the door.

Lonny shuffled into the apartment, their old apartment. He took off his coat and put it where the coat rack used to be. It fell to the floor.

"Is the kid asleep?" he whispered.

She froze. Eyes wide and mouth stricken.

Lonny sat on the couch, slipped off his shoes. Just like the old days.

"You are a sight for sore eyes, darling. I had me a day."

She wiped at her tears. Could he really be that drunk? Could booze bring their child back to life, their marriage?

"There are some terrible people in this world, my dear, and it's my job…."

"To put them away," she said softly, remembering him saying it a thousand times.

"Huh?"

"It's your job to put them away," she repeated. "Somebody's gotta clean up our fair city."

Lonny smiled. "Keep it safe."

"For the kids," they both whispered at the same time.

The tears had reached her mouth and she tasted the salt. Shut up, she thought, please shut up. But God, let's pretend, just for tonight. The loneliness of her life was like a burning building she didn't want to go into. Not tonight. Not alone.

She stood in front of Lonny. "Did you miss me?"

She pulled off her top.

Lonny squinted up at her, mouth and eyes crooked. She tried to picture her old Dylan. Her sweet Dylan. Her Saint Dylan, she used to call him when he worked too hard.

"You have no idea." He was up, and almost fell but she guided him.

His cold hands turned her skin to goose flesh. She tore his shirt off, and her raised nipples grazed his bare chest

"It's been too long," he said.

She kissed his gasoline breath, hungry for the heat there.

It took a while to get him ready for her. She writhed on top of him, his fingers explored, squeezed. She ground against him as her hands clawed his chest. Too long since she felt this. She moved faster. Then faster. Her breathing, short gasps as she rocked herself to that sweet, quivering place, and she screamed as every inch of her shook.

Then she opened her eyes to meet Dylan's dead, drunk eyes. Eyes that would remember none of this. Eyes that, right now, didn't remember the disappearance of their child. And when he did, he'd try to chase those memories away with a bottle of whiskey.

He was out cold in seconds.

She cried herself to sleep on his chest.

## 15

In the streets, the war began.

Messengers from both the Scarlotti and Denatale families had been sent to Providence, to obtain permission to kill the other's boss.

In a restaurant in Federal Hill, old men listened to conflicting positions. The old men sighed and sipped their espressos or their Sambucas.

The messengers waited.

The old men had seen these things before, these blood feuds. Better to end it quickly.

The oldest patriarch there finally cleared his throat and told the messengers, the families had one week to sort this out. After that, it would be sorted out for them.

So it began.

One of Red's biggest earners was gunned down in the front room of La Famiglia. Early the next morning, a child found three dead drug dealers in the playground across from Joe's American Bar and Grill.

The North End was turning into the Wild West, and Hanover Street became the Mason Dixon line. Scarlotti controlled the south, Denatale the north.

Angelo's son explained all of this to his father, who only nodded.

"What does the German have to say?"

The younger Denatale grinned. "Apparently Red hired a private investigator."

Angelo's brow wrinkled. "What for?"

"To find his son."

"Who took him?"

"PI thinks Kat's got him."

Angelo made a noise with his lips. "What's that dame up to?"

## 16

The boy was making Kat nervous.

Christopher wanted to talk to his parents. He was worried about them. She was not used to this. Protection was not her thing. Offense not defense was her thing. This kid was a liability, made her weaker, slower. But she'd made up her mind. Nothing was going to happen to this child. Not while she was alive.

The idea of being hunted unnerved the huntress.

She was in one of her safe houses, an apartment in Chestnut Hill. Just a few miles away, but it felt like a different planet here. A world of brick mansions and luxury shopping, Range Rovers, men in suits, women with stiff jaws and perfect hair. A place where people didn't look at faces, just clothes and cars.

Kat tried to visualize an end game she could live with.

Her best-case scenarios involved a lot of dead bodies. Her worst-case scenario included hers, too. She refused to imagine anything happening to Christopher.

"Do you think my parents are okay?"

"I know they are."

"How?"

"People like your parents, something happens to them, it makes the news."

So they watched the news.

Bad idea.

"Hey, that guy was at my birthday party. Remember?"

The title of the segment was "Mob War?" Kat winced when the reporter said, "Scarlotti crime family."

War, Kat thought sadly. And I'm on babysitting duty. The segment ended. "See," she said. "Mom and Dad are okay."

Christopher shot Kat a skeptical look.

Kat remembered hearing about her father. From her mother. He was a son of a bitch, but it had still rocked her world. In her imagination, it had always been Kat who did the deed, to protect her mother. Kat knew how something like that could affect a kid. She didn't want that for Christopher.

# 17

She was gone when Lonny woke up. The day hit him like a knee to the groin.

His head was full of exclamations, his hangover a swarm of hornets buzzing every inch of him. Naked, he lurched pathetically to the bathroom and vomited his soul into the toilet. The cool of the porcelain was the only mercy granted.

Pathetic.

He stared at the guilty face in the mirror.

Wretched.

It took all his strength not to take a swing.

He dressed, trying to remember more than a glimpse of his ex-wife's kindnesses last night, but it was all fleeting.

He went home, head buzzing, conscience throbbing, partly over last night but mostly over the still missing boy. Christopher needed rescuing. Lonny couldn't save himself.

His German shadow followed.

He had received his instructions.

Find the boy. Kill the girl.

Boy alive. Girl dead.

The German was not a kidnapper and was not happy. He did not enjoy having to be careful. But he understood the usefulness of a captive.

A thought occurred to him. A plan. A means of applying pressure. If needed, he thought. Let's see where this man takes us first.

It was early and cold. The detective pulled his jacket tight as he walked through the empty cobblestone streets of Quincy Market. Just a handful of cars as he crossed to Government Center and climbed the steps next to it. The German followed him into a T station and descended a steep staircase to the tracks. There were only three or four other people waiting for a train. The German sat and glanced around. But not at the man he was following until a train arrived and they both got on.

The detective got off at Kenmore Square.

He walked past Fenway Park and cut through a large parking lot to get to Audobon Circle, an apartment just off Beacon Street.

The German trailed a safe distance, but clearly the detective had other things on his mind. Several times, he had to stop to cough and spit something to the ground.

The detective looked cold and weak, ashamed. Vulnerable. The German wondered if this drunk would be of any use to him.

Then he saw something he couldn't believe.

There were a few people in the North End who knew Whitey was still alive. They told him about Lonagan.

Christ. Not now, Lonagan.

Whitey needed him clean and sober. He decided to go explain this to Lonagan. He knew where the detective lived.

Christopher was not sleeping well.

Nightmares.

But he no longer dreamed of monsters, under his bed or in the closet. Gone were the snakes and spiders and creepy crawly creatures of even six months ago.

Now he dreamed of men. With guns. Dreamed of heads exploding, heads he knew, his Aunt Kat, his Uncle Whitey, his father, his mother.

He woke screaming.

His Aunt Kat would be there, with a hand on his head, fingers brushing through his hair. A soothing "Shh" on her lips.

His tears shamed him. He wanted to be tough and brave like her, like his uncle, like his dad. Brave. But he was scared and knew if not for his Aunt Kat's protection he would be dead.

Like his Uncle Whitey.

Nobody really talked about what happened. When asked, grown-ups looked sideways, avoided the question. A better place, his father said.

"Heaven?" Christopher asked.

His father would look away, and almost smile. "Not quite."

He was dreaming again. A man, a bad man, in black clothes was shaking him.

No, it was Aunt Kat.

"Hey, Christopher," she said and stroked his cheek. "We gotta get up, buddy."

It was early. The dimmest of light through the bedroom window, the world just a sketch, an outline without colors.

"Okay?"

"Okay." He nodded. "Where are we going?"

"To see a man I know."

"Who?"

"Someone who might help us."

Might? Christopher thought.

She smiled at him. "You'll like him. He used to have a boy your age."

He used to be a hero, she thought. He used to save people.

# 18

Lonny knew there was someone else in his apartment.

Something was off, a scent, a sound.

He drew his pistol.

Strong hands squeezed around his other arm, like a vice around his wrist. Panic seized his insides just as hard.

"Easy, Lonagan. It's Whitey." He let him go.

"Motherfucker," Lonny spat.

He walked to the kitchen. A bottle of water in the fridge. "Just getting in?"

"You got something to say, Whitey?"

"I need you to hold it together."

Lonny closed his eyes and drank.

Whitey studied him.

Lonny wiped his mouth with his sleeve. "Where would she go?"

"How the fuck—"

"You taught her, right? Taught her everything she knows. Where would she go?"

"Out of the state. Out of the country. But the kid throws everything off."

"How?"

"With the kid, you're more vulnerable, slower, easier to spot."

"What the hell is she doing with that kid?"

Whitey shook his head. "Hey, watch out for a guy. Blond hair. Blue eyes. They call him the German."

A face appeared to Lonny from the night before. "What about him?"

"He works for Denatale. I caught him tailing me last night."

Lonny tried to put the face in context, but it would only float, isolated in the murk. "Does he have a scar right here?" Lonny touched the side of his face.

Whitey nodded. "You too, huh?"

A knock on the door.

Whitey's pistol was in his hand.

Lonny quietly stepped to the door, looked through the peephole, thinking, please be Kelly, please be Kelly.

Kat Scarlotti's serious face stared back at him. Next to her, the boy, Christopher.

Lonny leaned his head against the door,

"What's up?" Whitey whispered.

"Put that piece away."

"What?"

"Holster it."

Reluctantly, Whitey did as he was told.

Lonny took a deep breath and opened the door.

"Lonny, I need your—" she started to say then her jaw turned slack and useless.

"Uncle Whitey?" Christopher's eyes sprang wide, joy spreading over his entire face as he ran to him.

Whitey spread his arms and picked the boy up in a bear hug. "Christ, look at the size of you."

"Everyone said you were dead."

"Ha!" Whitey said. "Man hasn't been born who could put me down."

"Aunt Kat can you believe it?"

"No," she said. "I can't."

She hadn't moved a muscle.

Christopher ran back to her and pulled her inside the apartment. Her eyes never left Whitey.

"You're a son of a bitch, William Scarlotti."

Lonny was poised. Ready to block an attack. Not sure who it would come from.

"Me? I'm the bad guy?"

"You were always the bad guy. Like the kid said, you were dead. But you weren't, were you? You might have told your wife. The love of your life. Oh, but maybe you did. Maybe that's not the same person."

"They wouldn't let me contact anyone."

"Since when do you take orders?" she whispered, then shouted, "Since when?"

Whitey looked at Christopher.

The boy seemed utterly lost. Lonny knew how he felt.

"Look what happened when you found me."

A sad smile as she shook her head. "You're not just a son of a bitch. You're a stupid son of a bitch, William Scarlotti."

"That girl didn't deserve—"

"You made that choice when you invited her into your life. And don't you dare talk to me about deserve."

Whitey's face turned red, then purple.

"I wasn't paid to hit her. The Denatale's wanted you. If it wasn't me, you'd be dead."

"You want I should thank you?"

"You think you can just start over? Become someone new? You think you're some kind of dirty saint that can still get into Heaven?"

Whitey's eyes burned. Maybe that was what he thought.

"Put yourself in my position, Whitey. What would you have done? What would the *old* Whitey have done, the *real* Whitey? The killer. The man I loved.

Whitey trembled with emotion.

Kat came closer to him. "Do you remember what you taught me? Everyone is expendable." Her eyes were shiny with tears. "Everyone but us. Remember? It was us against the world."

Whitey cleared his throat. "I remember."

A gunshot.

Broken glass.

Kat. In the chest.

The speed of Whitey's return shot, as fast as a cobra strike.

Whitey glanced at Lonny, who realized, as if waking from a dream, that he had pushed Christopher to the floor and was covering him with his own body. Lonny nodded. "Go get him."

Whitey squatted next to Kat, took her hand. "Everyone but us," he said and kissed her lips.

Then he was out the screen door and over the railing.

More gunshots.

Lonny moved over to Kat. She knew what Lonny knew. She was acquainted with deadly wounds. He put a pillow over the hole in her chest. She hugged it.

Christopher knelt next to her.

"It's okay, Aunt Kat. This is just one of my dreams. I'm gonna wake up any second."

A smile trembled on Kat's lips. The expression in her eyes, a look Lonny knew so well; it was the look of breaking someone's heart. She reached for Christopher, who took her hand, those deadly hands, which never touched anything so gently.

Lonny clasped the boy's neck. "Kiss her goodbye, Christopher."

A flash of gratitude on her face. "Take good care," she whispered to Lonny, the blood filling her lungs. She coughed.

"I will," Lonny said.

"Don't trust her," she said.

"Who?"

"Tell Whitey…." Her eyes drifted.

"I will," Lonny said. "But he already knows."

The last breath shuddered out of her. Lonny watched her eyes as they froze on her nephew. Lonny couldn't help but notice, she made a very pretty corpse.

The German had seen a light go on. On the third floor. After the girl and the boy went in, the German climbed up the side of the building.

Easy enough. Plenty of big brick blocks to hold onto.

He moved slowly.

At this hour, the street was quiet. A handful of pedestrians. None looking up.

He pulled himself over the deck's metal railing, fingers still cold even through his gloves.

He watched the heated exchange of the Italian couple, the killers. He let her speak her piece.

Aimed.

Fired.

A blur of movement, a blink, and the German's shoulder exploded with pain. He went over the railing, caught the next floor's railing, then dropped to the pavement, his ankle twisting. He limp-ran down the street.

Above him, a sliding door opened with a splash of glass falling.

A bullet missed him by an inch. Maybe less.

The German lurched into an alley. Knew he had only moments to save himself.

A poor unsuspecting fool, a man in a suit, an agent of the devil, was unlocking his car. A German sedan. He was still, frozen by the sound of the gun firing.

The German raised his pistol. "The keys," he said.

The man dropped them on the seat.

The German shot him in the head. The man nodded stupidly, as if he was in agreement with everything happening, then collapsed. The German slipped into the car and started the engine.

Whitey saw him duck into the alley. He knew another route, and sprinted down a different alley, ran around an apartment building. Heard the crack of a bullet. One more poor bastard down.

He emerged into the German's alley. Saw the stockbroker or lawyer or accountant on the ground. Saw the German at the wheel, waiting.

Whitey crept up to the car.

Sirens in the distance.

A woman came out of a door. She squinted at the man lying in the street, then at Whitey, pistol in hand, and she screamed.

The German turned and saw Whitey. Punched the gas.

Whitey opened fire. Two tires popped. The back window shattered. He emptied his clip. The car skidded on metal rims, turned the corner and sped away.

The woman who had screamed remained frozen on the sidewalk like a scared statue.

Whitey sighed. "Call the police," he said.

The German was easy for the police to spot, sparks flying from the metal rims grinding pavement. He saw the flashing lights in his rearview. One cruiser, then another.

They were on a bridge.

The German squeezed the steering wheel as he braked.

When the first cruiser was even with him on his right, the German stomped the gas pedal and turned the wheel into the squad car. The cruiser jumped the Jersey barrier and punched a hole in the chain link fence, and then tumbled, nose first, onto the Mass Pike.

The German swerved back onto the road and slammed on the brakes.

In a blur he was out the passenger door, gun drawn, before the other cruiser had even stopped or realized he'd left.

The officers opened their car doors, buzzing on adrenaline and fear, their heads full of curses to scream but mouths stuttering in rage and shock.

Then the German came out of nowhere, like a bird of prey; and there were two more cop widows in Boston, three more orphans.

Cars were piled on both sides of the bridge, plenty of witnesses to interview, a glorious confusion for the police to try and make sense of. The German grinned as he scaled the fence and leapt half a story to a courtyard below. The landing made him cry out. Then he vanished into the swarms of students crowding the campus of Boston University.

He sent a text. "Finished with woman, pursuing child, sorry for mess."

Whitey remembered the last time he had spoken to his brother, face to face.

"Sooner or later," Whitey said, "Angelo will make his move."

"So let's make ours."

Whitey shook his head. They were in Red's office, what used to be their father's office. Whitey liked that his brother was here, that his family was here. He needed to protect them. "Our move is, I turn state's evidence."

"Go G?"

Whitey nodded.

"Doesn't really seem like your style."

"Maybe it's time to change my style. I'm not getting any younger."

Red looked at the chessboard between them and smiled a toothless smile. Lately, his brother's game had gotten more conservative. They both knew this was the best plan, but neither wanted to do it. For one simple reason. They would miss each other. They knew how rare it was to have someone who knew you so completely. That's not what wives were for.

"And Kat?"

"Nobody can know."

"You've already talked to the Feds."

It wasn't a question. Whitey said nothing.

"Things used to be a lot simpler, didn't they?" Red said.

Whitey shrugged. "We knew less. That didn't make things simple."

"Yes, it did."

Yes it did, Whitey thought. He sat on a bench inside a small, gated playground across from Joe's American Bar and Grille. The playscape and swings were crowded with kids, like ants on a dead animal. Nannies with strollers chatted while they supervised the mayhem. Whitey was filled with the typical envy adults have watching kids play. Whitey tried to imagine them grown up, picked out the bullies, the cowards, the sluts, the princesses.

A man in a dark suit opened the gate, alone, no children. His brother. Red sat on the same bench as Whitey.

"I'm sorry about Kat."

"Christopher is okay."

Red closed his eyes, Whitey knew, to force back the tears. "Where?"

"With Lonagan."

Red nodded. "I thought maybe…. I remember Christopher loved this park."

"It's not safe," Whitey said.

"Denatale?"

Whitey nodded. "Who knew, Richard? About me?"

"I knew. But I didn't know everything, did I?"

Whitey had to look away from his brother, back at the children. He tried to pick out the future adulterers. "You knew everything you needed to know."

Red nodded. "You were protecting me. Yeah?"

"Yeah." The lie died on his tongue. The hair on the back of Whitey's neck tingled. He scanned the crowds for the well-dressed Vincent. Braced himself for the sound and feel of a bullet. Sweat beaded on his face.

"I should have sent Kat up to kill you."

"You didn't?"

"Are you dead?"

"So who knew?"

"The Feds."

"Anyone else?"

Red smiled. A smile that had nothing to do with happiness.

"Who?"

"My wife."

Whitey sighed. "Things used to be a lot simpler."

Linda Scarlotti, the only addiction Whitey ever had. She was like China White heroin. He was hooked after the first taste. Like any junky, he couldn't get enough, would take silly chances just for an hour alone with her. With Kat, everything was rough and hard. With Linda, it was soft and easy. Linda was the yin to Kat's yang. Just thinking about her could make him shudder with withdrawal as he pictured her long, lean, freckled body, the beautiful, quivering paleness of her.

"Do you ever wish it was you?"

He had to concentrate to hear what she said when she was naked. "What?"

She dragged her index finger down his chest. "Running things. Do you ever wish it was you?"

"Never."

It was the last question she ever asked him. She had left in a hurry, her lips like sharp icicles as she kissed him goodbye.

After she was gone, he was afraid. Afraid of what she might make him do, what he might be willing to do if she withheld herself from him.

That was when he came up with his plan. He needed to go away, forever.

## 19

Vilma lived near Northeastern, in the Fens off Huntington Avenue. She was a professor of Latin America studies. Lonny had never been to her home before, but she had described it enough times to make it easy for him to find.

In a daze Christopher followed as Lonny knocked on her door.

The sound of her footsteps inside. "Hold on," her voice called. More footsteps and the door opened.

"Dylan?" She sounded more curious than surprised. Vilma had been through enough not to let an unexpected visit from a friend distress her. "Come by for a game?"

"I wish."

"Who is this?" Christopher said from behind Lonny.

She squinted at the boy. "*Ah, y que es esto? Como te llamas, chico?*"

"Christopher, this is Vilma. Vilma, Christopher. Christopher Scarlotti."

The last name caused her eyes to widen. She appeared to be doing some calculations in her head. "How long?"

Lonny sighed. "A day? Give or take."

"Please come in, you two."

"I need to use the bathroom," Christopher said.

"At the end of the hall my little amigo."

When the bathroom door shut, Vilma said, "The boy is in danger?"

"Yes."

"You are in danger?"

"Yes."

"How exciting."

"I'm sorry to put you in this position, Vilma."

She smiled, then she looked concerned. "How was your fall?"

"Come again?"

"Off the wagon?"

Lonny looked away from her. "Hard."

She nodded. "*Esta bien, amigo.* Not today and not tomorrow. Okay?"

He swallowed. "Okay."

The toilet flushed.

"And Vilma?"

"Si?"

"The boy has been through some awful things today."

She grimaced. "I understand. You be careful."

Christopher came out of the bathroom. His eye caught the wooden chess set on the kitchen table. The pieces reminded Lonny of the Easter Island statues or totem pole faces.

"Do you play, Christopher?" Vilma asked.

The boy touched one of the pawns and nodded.

"Then we will get along just fine."

"Christopher," Lonny said, "I'll be back as soon as I can."

Christopher looked nervously at Lonny. "Does she have a gun?"

She chuckled. "Vilma does not need guns to scare people off."

Christopher looked skeptical.

# 20

Kelly thought about calling him all day. What would she say? She wasn't sure how she felt about what had happened last night. Hadn't realized how hungry she was for human contact, for intimacy.

It had stirred up memories, good and bad.

Still, wasn't that better than the numbness her life had become? A daily avoidance of feeling. Wasn't that what Dylan's drinking was about, numbness? We all chased our demons away, however we could.

She opened the door to her apartment building, stopped at the mailbox, while an inner debate raged over whether to call him. A list of the things she missed did battle with the list of the things she didn't. Dylan Thomas Lonagan was a coin and you never knew which side he would land on, Jekyll or Hyde.

In her apartment, she set the mail on the dining room table, flipped on the light, and froze.

A man was sitting in her leather chair.

She screamed.

He held a silver handgun in his right hand, and casually pointed it at her. He put a finger to his lips. "Shh."

She recognized him. The blond man from the night before, with Dylan. He looked a bit like the new James Bond actor. In this light his eyes appeared colorless, his expression blank, cruel, comfortably numb.

She was having trouble breathing. "What? What do you want?"

He blinked and said, "I want you to call Dylan Lonagan."

An accent. German?

Lonny was in the Boston Commons, near the swan boats, when his cell buzzed. He recognized her number.

"I was kind of hoping you'd call," he said.

"Dylan, I don't know what's happening."

The panic in her voice was like fingers around his heart.

"What is it?" He knew, but hoped he was wrong.

At first, he thought he lost the connection. No, she was crying, or trying very hard not to. "There's a man. With a gun."

Lonny stopped walking. "Where are you?"

"Ah, Herr Lonagan," a new voice said. The German. The ice in his voice made Lonny shiver. "Never mind about where we are."

"What do you want?"

"The boy."

"A trade?"

"A fair trade, no?"

"Where?"

"Quincy Market. The north steps."

"When?"

"One hour."

"What if—"

"Enough. You know the answers to these questions. Bring the boy to the north steps. Leave him. The woman will be at the south steps. Understand?"

"Yes."

"Good. Keep your phone close. You will receive instructions."

*

The German put her phone in his pocket and sighed. He did not enjoy involving civilians in his work. Too unpredictable. He stood.

"You heard?"

The woman nodded. Beneath the fatigue and the fear she was quite beautiful.

"Do what you are told and everything will be fine for you and Dylan."

"Who is the boy?"

The German punched her, hard, in the stomach. She crumpled to the ground, gasping for breath.

"The boy does not concern you. You will ask no questions. You will do as you are told. Understand?"

The woman nodded and wept.

So beautiful. Such a waste.

"Sit, please."

She did it quickly, like a well-trained dog, eager to please.

The German nodded in approval. He lifted a case and opened it. His long-range rifle. A DSR-50. He had never missed with it. He quickly checked all the parts, made sure he had his .50 caliber bullets. Then he closed and latched the case. As always, he felt comforted by the sight of the well-oiled machine.

The boy would not be there. The German understood this. A clean shot at Lonagan was all he wanted. Perhaps the Italian would be there as well. Then this woman, unfortunate, but necessary. No loose ends.

Then the German could locate the boy. With no interference.

*

Whitey answered on the first ring.

"Trouble?" he said.

"The German," Lonny said. "He has my wife."

Whitey absorbed this, then said, "And he wants to trade."

"Yes. For the boy."

"He can't have the boy."

"I know that."

"Good. Where's the meet?"

"Quincy Market. The north steps." Lonny rubbed his face, tried to control the panic buzzing at the back of his brain.

"Where does she live?"

"Beacon Hill."

"Okay. We've got time."

"For what?"

"Where are you?"

"Northeastern."

Whitey's heart surged as he explained how to proceed. The life of a hero, he thought. Someone needed saving and Lonagan had called Whitey.

The German and Kelly walked from her apartment. It was a frigid day. The wind bit at the tears in her eyes.

There was no talking. They both knew the way.

The German kept his hands in his pockets. His right hand held a small firearm. Smaller than anything Dylan had owned. But in the bag over his shoulder was the biggest rifle she'd ever seen.

"You will wait at the steps. If you leave—" the German shrugged apologetically— "I must kill the boy. And your Dylan."

My Dylan, she thought and sighed.

They passed a policeman.

Kelly tensed as if she might not be able to control herself.

The German smiled, as if amused by her thoughts.

They walked. Past the old capitol building with its gold dome shining. To their right, in the Boston Commons, Kelly could see a skating rink, could hear the sounds of children on the ice. Cruel noises to her ears.

They took a left through Suffolk University. College kids rushed to class, their breath steaming from their mouths.

None of them knew, not a soul, how much trouble she was in, how dangerous the blond man next to her was.

How could they?

Lonny spotted them, walking past Government Center.

He dialed Whitey. Herd ringing in his earpiece.

"Go," Whitey said.

"I've got them. Coming down the steps next to Government Center."

As Lonny watched, a crowd of business folk crossed in front of them. The German was gone. Kelly kept walking down the steps.

"Dammit, I just lost him."

"I've got him. Go get Kelly out of here."

Lonny stepped out of the coffee shop, scanning the crowd for either the German or Whitey. Both were ghosts. Instead, he spotted Vincent, Red's well-dressed lieutenant.

Kelly was halfway down the steps.

Vincent was moving away, back turned to Lonny. He moved like he dressed. Smooth, elegant, gliding through the thickening crowd like a dancer. He did nothing to call attention to himself.

Over Vincent's shoulder, Lonny spotted Whitey, who was as engaged as Vincent on his prey. Eyes locked on his target.

It was almost comical, this chain of armed men, and the unsuspecting commuters surrounding them, walking home half asleep, on auto pilot. They were in for a rude awakening.

Lonny had his gun in his hand and was considered firing into the air when Vincent aimed his pistol at Whitey. No more thinking, just action. Lonny's bullet found the center of Vincent's back. He crumpled.

The commuter zombies woke up, turned into a panicked mob, running, screaming.

Whitey had Lonny in his sights, then lowered his weapon. He briefly looked at Vincent, then back at Lonny.

Lonny was frozen. His joints had locked and his eyes did not blink, could not stop staring at the first man he had ever killed.

The serene evening commute turned into a riot. One woman looked down at the blood that had spilled from Vincent onto her pretty, blue overcoat, howling as if she had been shot.

Lonny's eyes took it all in.

Vincent's trembling hands.

His body twisting, head angling to see his executioner.

His eyes found Lonny's, a recognition, before they turned into hazel marbles.

Whitey's hand on Lonny's shoulder. His voice, calm, clear, in Lonny's ear.

"We need to get Kelly."

She heard the gunshot. She had never heard a gun shot in real life before, but the report was unmistakable. Who was dead?

The boy?

Dylan?

Or had Dylan turned the tables on the German?

Should she go back? Should she still go to the steps? Frightened people ran past her, shoved, tripped. She held onto the railing of the stairs, leaned on it as more tears welled in her eyes.

She fought with herself, but after a moment she turned and rushed, against the current, back up the stairs.

Her skin tingled. She imagined the German watching her through the scope on his rifle, thought about his finger on the trigger. She shivered.

At the top of the steps, she saw Dylan rushing toward her.

And she heard screaming. A woman was screaming. A beautiful woman with red hair was screaming, it seemed, right at Kelly.


The German was long gone. But Linda Scarlotti was watching Kelly with her finger on a trigger.

This was not how it was supposed to go. Nothing had happened the way it was supposed to.

Whitey was supposed to be dead. A gift for the Denatales. A show of good faith.

And Vincent was supposed to be the one to find the boy. Her husband's trusted general. But no, Red had to go outside the family and find this drunk shamus, like a dog with a bone, who just wouldn't stop sniffing. Kat had called an audible up in Vermont. At least she'd got what she deserved.

Mrs. Scarlotti pictured the tangled web she had constructed, now torn apart.

The only one caught in it was her.

And now her Vincent, her man, was dead.

All because of that goddamned Lonagan.

That's what she was shouting, "Lonagan!" As she pulled her dainty .22 out of her pocket and pointed it (like it's your finger, Vincent told her) at Lonagan's ex-wife.

"Lonagan!"

She was close enough to smell the bitch's scent. Estee Lauder and fear.

Lonny could not understand what he was seeing. His wife and Red's wife and a gun. Still shaking with adrenaline, Lonny thought of Red's son; this had the feel of a dream. It was nothing like real life.

"Lonagan!" Mrs. Scarlotti shouted, her face a twisted, ugly sneer.

Then Whitey dropped her with a bullet to the head.

More chaos as the crowd screamed and scattered, unsure where to go now.

"Where is Christopher?" Whitey asked Lonny.

Kelly threw up all over the steps. The vomit steamed in the frigid air.

Lonny knelt next to her. "Northeastern. Just before the museum. With Vilma."

# 21

She knew.

Before the door opened. Before she saw the blond man's face. She often claimed a supernatural awareness, a sixth sense if you like.

She knew when bad things were going to happen, even as a child.

In Guatemala, in her youth, she had known when the dark mood was about to descend on her father, possess him. She knew to be still, to avoid his eyes, his dark, dark eyes.

Her brothers never saw it coming. They paid for their ignorance, with pain.

And her mother, Vilma had known what she would do to him. She still kept that secret locked in her heart.

So she knew, when she heard those soft, slow footsteps in her hallway, that the boy was in trouble.

They were playing chess. It seemed to soothe him. The game soothed her too. The boy wasn't bad. He had foresight, thought a few moves ahead, so rare in boys, rarer still in men.

A sad smile on her face as he took her queen and looked at her proudly. Men could never resist that trap.

She was hoping to teach him a lesson.

But then she heard, and knew, so instead she leaned close and whispered, "Time to run, Christopher. Out the window."

*

The German was surprised to find the door unlocked. He chuckled to himself as he pushed it open.

The woman nodded at him. She was sitting at a table in the kitchen, a chess set in front of her. The game had not started.

He did not see the boy, did not hear him, but he could smell him.

She motioned to the board. "Do you play?"

The question caught him so off guard, he smiled and nodded.

She pointed to the chair across from her. "Sit."

He sat. It was a beautiful, wooden chess set. Absently, he touched the king, stroked it.

The woman looked at him with amusement. No fear. She was no killer but she knew he was. And still no fear. He was impressed.

"If you're in a hurry," she said as she pulled something from under the table, "we could play a timed match."

A small box with two clocks. She clicked her side and moved her queen's pawn to Q4, then smacked the button on her clock again.

The German was on the clock. He realized with something like shock that he was still smiling. He moved his king's knight and hit the timer.

The game had begun.

He was not used to being on the clock, but he was good.

When she took his knight, after a vigorous chase, he knocked the table in acknowledgment. When she tried to snare him, he did not take the bait, but left her queen be. She winked at him.

He was the better player. Went right for the jugular. A killer in every way.

When it was clear to both of them, she knocked her king over in resignation.

He nodded. "You enjoy the game, not so much winning."

Her teeth flashed. The joy of being understood. A wonderful final thought, he decided, and ended her life with a burp from his silenced revolver.

Regret was a rare emotion from him, he did not enjoy the throbbing now in his tiny, cold heart, but there it was, unexpected and unwelcome.

He closed her eyes with his fingers and sighed.

The German looked in the other rooms. In one, an open window let in a biting breeze. He looked outside. No sign, the boy was in the wind.

## 22

When Lonny and Whitey got to Vilma's apartment, the door was unlocked, the apartment cold, and another dead woman greeted them in the kitchen.

Lonny saw the chess set in front of her and flipped it over.

"Stop," Whitey said. "We need to find Christopher."

Lonny shook with rage, but quieted.

They found the open window.

"She stalled him." Lonny smiled tightly.

"While Christopher went out the window?"

"That's what she told him to do." Lonny walked over to the closet, a thoughtful expression on his face. "But kids don't always listen." Lonny opened the closet door.

A trembling Christopher peered up at them.

"It's okay." Lonny knew it was a lie, but wasn't sure what else to say.

The boy looked feral, lost. Lonny remembered, as a child, when a squirrel had climbed into his family's chimney. Christopher reminded him of that scared squirrel. He had fallen down a rabbit hole into a frightening world of creatures he had previously only seen from afar.

"Christopher?" Whitey said.

The boy's mouth quivered until his voice cracked. "Uncle Whitey?"

"Stay where you are, kid."

The boy nodded.

Whitey looked at Lonny. "He's still out there. He'll wait for us to leave."

"What's our move?" Lonny gazed out the open window, looking absently for the German assassin.

There was a flash across the street and then Whitey knocked Lonny to the floor and a bullet hole appeared on the wall.

"Stay with the boy," Whitey said.

Lonny wanted to argue but knew it was the right play. This was Whitey's battle to win or lose.

Whitey rushed over to the closet. "Christopher, I need you to be brave for me. I need you to listen to Lonny."

Christopher nodded.

"I'm gonna take care of the bad man."

"Get him good, Uncle Whitey."

Whitey kissed his nephew on the forehead. The look in his eyes when he touched Lonny's shoulder made the former detective shiver as Whitey's expression changed from affection to the hardness of a born killer. The man who left that room had only one thing on his mind: vengeance.

The German was furious. He had revealed his position and hadn't killed anyone. He pressed a button on his phone.

"The boy is probably on his way home. Perhaps you have men to watch for him?"

He did not wait for a reply.

The German knew the Italian would come for him. The detective would pursue the boy. A killer and a protector by nature.

Whitey was scared.

He stood in the lobby of Vilma's building sucking air into his lungs. He needed to cross the street and he wanted the

German to take a shot at him, reveal his location. Was he in the same room? More than anything, Whitey needed the German to miss.

He inhaled, opened the door and poked his head out and pulled it in. No shot. He ran outside. He stopped, stutter stepped, faked left, and then went right. He pictured himself in the German's crosshairs, tried to time how long it would take to line up the shot. With every step, he bet his life.

Cars swerved around him, slammed on their brakes, honking. Pedestrians squinted in his direction.

His entire body clenched, braced for the German's bullet. It didn't come.

The German watched it all through his rifle lens, a tight smile of respect on his lips. It was rare that the German came up against a worthy adversary. Now today, two. The woman with the chess set and this Italian. Nice to deal with people who knew and accepted the stakes of the contest. Life and death. The only stakes worth playing for.

The Italian would not allow the German to get comfortable; three times the German thought he might have him but then a twitch of movement would throw him off. So be it. Now the Italian wouldn't know the whereabouts of the German, who could exploit his opponent's uncertainty.

He remembered Afghanistan. The helicopter crash, into the side of a mountain. He remembered everything constricting, his gut, his chest, even his heart, before impact. Fear, an unfamiliar sensation. The pilot had been crushed in the cockpit, two others impaled by glass and metal.

Scraped and bruised, but alive, he checked on the dead soldiers before grabbing his rifle and jogging to higher ground.

Five Afghanis coming for him, and when they moved through open sand, they had moved with the same herky-jerky movement as Scarlotti. The younger German had fired, but hit nothing, five times, bullets he couldn't spare, and now they knew exactly where he was.

He returned to the helicopter, and wiped more blood on himself from his platoon mates, rubbing the sticky fluid onto his face, the rusty smell overpowering. He sat. He waited.

Not very long.

They were quiet, fast, securing the area. They inspected the helicopter. The German watched, eyes wide and dead, careful not to move his pupils. Using his peripheral vision, he braced for a bullet from their American-supplied weapons. That tight feeling, fear.

It was there in the helicopter, playing dead. He knew he wouldn't be following anyone's orders again.

Their voices rose with the belief that the shooter had fled. The German waited, not sure what to do, not sure where he was. One Afghani was going through the pockets of the pilot, gathering his weapons and throwing them to the soldiers outside.

Then the radio crackled to life and the German turned toward the sound, and the young Afghani in the cockpit noticed. It was the last thing he would ever notice. The German's bullet hit him in the left cheek, the ones outside, he hit in the chest.

There were two more, about twenty meters away. They panicked, opened fire on the helicopter. The German felt a stab of pain in his arm, just below his shoulder. But he remained calm. One never knew until the moment was upon them, if he could be cool under fire.

The German was cool. Carefully he lined up a shot and fired a burst at the closest soldier. He didn't miss.

The last soldier continued the panic of gunfire as the German crawled into the cockpit, over twisted metal and shattered glass, reaching for the radio. English sounded so precise compared to the sing-song gibberish of these soldiers. "Hang in there," the British officer told him. "We are en route."

The German waited and observed the soldier firing at him. A pattern emerged and the German knew when the man would pop up and fire, and the German readied the .45 bullet to be waiting for him when he did.

He'd been lucky. Those men had been too young, too green. When the moment came, they had panicked, been sloppy.

He knew William Scarlotti was none of these things. He tried to shake it off but that was like shaking off smoke, the now familiar, unwelcome sensation of fear squeezing his chest.

The trick, Whitey thought, was to assume you were going to die. It freed up your mind to worry about other things. It was amazing what you could accomplish when you weren't busy trying to save your life.

When you thought you were living your final moments, the world came into sharp focus. The details sang. This dim, quiet hallway would fit right into a Hitchcock film. The cigarette burns on the rug. The melody of street sounds, tires squealing, horns honking. You never knew what the last thing you were going to notice would be.

He gripped the pistol in his hand and tried the door to the apartment, the one the German had fired from. Unlocked. He pushed it open. It squealed on its hinges like something out of a slasher movie.

There was a woman slumped back in her chair in the kitchen, but Whitey didn't think about her; he saw Karen, shot between the eyes, in a triangle house in Vermont, dead before she knew what hit her, dead because of him, because he couldn't stay away. He might as well have pulled the trigger.

His heartbeat rang like a bell in his head. He felt heavy, like he was underwater, limbs moving through liquid.

Some sins you never stopped paying for.

Why was she holding a gun?

For half a second, he thought it was her ghost, come back from the dead to exact revenge. For half a second, he was ready to accept his punishment. Then instinct took over. He shot the corpse, right through her heart, and heard a man curse in German.

Whitey didn't realize at first that he had been hit in his left arm, a glancing blow. He was too busy admiring his opponent. The German had put his arm though the sleeve of the woman's sweater. She was on his lap. He seemed to hold her tenderly.

Then the pain in his arm made him suck in his breath. He found a towel to press on the wound.

"Almost." He touched the dead man's shoulder. "Almost."

## 23

Angelo Denatale Junior was going to end this war today. Not any henchmen, not the German, not his father. Him. End it with a few well-placed bullets.

He would do what he had to do and leave no doubt who ran Boston's underworld. Him. Angelo Denatale Junior.

He dressed casual, stuffed the .45 into his jeans and covered it with a sweater, then put on an overcoat and a hat. When he stepped outside he didn't notice the cold, his blood the same temperature as the frigid air outside.

Lonny and the boy were on the trolley, the inbound E-Line. He was bone weary, fighting sleep, but every time it threatened to claim him, the face of the man, Vincent, was waiting for him. He observed the boy, who seemed to be in the midst of a similar struggle. The kid gazed out the window at a world filled with danger, with death. Lonny pictured the boy's mother and shuddered.

"Want to talk about it?"

The boy shook his head, then changed his mind. "Do you think Aunt Kat is in Heaven?"

The question knocked the wind out of him. "What do you think?"

The boy pressed his lips together and shook his head just slightly. He looked into Lonny's eyes. Lonny wanted to look away, but didn't.

"Is my dad a bad guy?"

Lonny looked up at the ceiling as the trolley ground through a turn underground, then he turned back at the boy. "How old are you?"

"Ten."

"You read a lot?"

The boy nodded.

"I suppose it's about time you learned."

"What?"

"Real life's not so much like books. Most people aren't just good or bad."

"What do you mean?"

"Sometimes good people do bad things."

The boy thought about that. "Like killing someone?"

"Sometimes."

"But you're a good guy."

"I try to be." He stopped. "I used to be."

"Aunt Kat said you were."

"Did she?"

"Yup." The boy seemed comforted by the memory. "Mr. Lonagan?"

"Call me Dylan."

"Why is there so much bad?"

What a terrible question to have to ask. "Nobody really knows, kid. But some people think this is all there is. No Heaven. No Hell. Just right now. Right here. And some of those people will do whatever they have to to get what they want. Money, power, you name it. For those people there are no rules. At least not the kind the rest of us play by."

Then Lonny thought about Whitey and Kat Scarlotti. "There are others who believe they are already damned and so it's hopeless."

"Can they be saved?"

"I hope so." Lonny touched the boy's shoulder. "This is our stop."

Almost home, Lonny wondered how Red would explain to Christopher what had happened to his mother. What would that do to this boy? What would happen to his heart? What would it turn this boy into? For a moment, Lonny didn't envy Red his son, his healthy, inquisitive boy and all the complications it brought.

"We're going home?" the boy said, hopefully.

And then the wound, the wound that never healed inside Lonny was ripped open again, and he would have done anything to have his son back. Anything. He nodded at Christopher and cleared his throat.

They were walking up Hanover Street, the trees bare in the brisk wind, the sidewalk awash in the smells of the North End, marinara sauces, olive oil, dough, the air a carnival for the nose.

Christopher seemed to relax at the familiar scents and sounds of home.

A block away, Lonny rang Red and told him he was bringing his son home.

They turned a corner and saw the tall, brick building, and Christopher broke into a run, his father at the front door, a rainbow of emotions splashed across his haggard face. By now the news about his wife had reached him, but seeing his son made joy win. A smile cracked his face in half.

Then Lonny noticed the car, a silver Mercedes. A man at the wheel. And he knew something was wrong.

Angelo Denatale Junior emerged from the driver's side wielding a hand cannon.

Lonny would never know who he was there to kill, maybe both of them. Lonny never hesitated, never doubted, guided by his new killer's instincts. Angelo never got a shot off. The three bullets were grouped perfectly around his heart.

# 24

Lonny didn't have to wait long for the police to show up. They barked orders and he followed them, put his gun on the ground, hands behind his head. Handcuffed, he took a ride to the station house. They brought him to a room with a one-way window. His reflection kept him company while he waited, and waited. Lonny knew the routine, would have done the same thing. Outside that room, the police had a lot of dots to connect and a trail of dead bodies to uncover.

Christopher was safe with his father. In the end, that was all he really cared about. He thought of the two men he had killed, now being poked and prodded and ripped apart in the coroner's lab, and he had no regrets.

Eventually, Lonny dozed.

He woke when the door opened, and Agent Riley entered.

The federal agent sat across from him and sighed like he was about to do something he didn't care for. "It's like the goddamned wild west out there today. Bodies all over the place." He folded his hands on the table, looked at Lonny. "Been reading ballistics reports all day."

That would tell quite a tale, Lonny thought.

"Places your gun at  several crimes scenes today. Not only did it take out the heir to the Denatale crime family, Angelo Junior. It also punched Vincent Gubatosi's ticket. Know him?"

Lonny only listened, waited. He'd been on the other side of this table before.

"Bit of a clothes horse, Vincent. Worked for Richard Scarlotti. Know him?"

"Everybody in Boston knows Richard Scarlotti."

Riley nodded. "It gets crazier though. We've got a woman's body in an apartment off Huntington, near the MFA, in her kitchen. One shot to the head. Looks like she lost a game of chess."

Lonny closed his eyes, but the image of Vilma, cold and dead, was all he could see.

"Now across the street there's another woman's body. Same gun killed her. Only she's sitting on a dead man's lap. Get this, he's holding the gun that killed both women. But not just them. Also two patrolmen smoked on Beacon Street in that crazy chase yesterday. The same gun—and here's the cherry on top—that iced Kat Scarlotti."

Was that only yesterday?

"Know who we think this guy is?"

"The German."

Riley scowled at Lonny. "That's right."

There was one more piece to this puzzle, Lonny knew. He waited for Riley to say it.

"Ballistics also tells us the bullet they took out of the German came from the same gun that took out Red Scarlotti's wife."

Riley watched Lonny's reaction.

"We both know who that was."

Lonny didn't move.

"If I *was* Whitey Scarlotti, I'd be a little worried about that information becoming public knowledge."

Lonny wondered how that would play out.

"The next time you see Whitey, tell him the federal government has no further need of his services."

*

Word of Angelo Junior's death traveled fast through the wiseguy network. When it reached the ears of the old family men in Federal Hill, a decision was reached.

The war was over. One more casualty. A mercy killing.

Angelo Senior took his nightly shower, his head twirling with the logistics of street warfare. Not an unpleasant sensation, battle brought out the best in Angelo. It was all a chess match. He was willing to trade pieces. The German for Kat Scarlotti. The trick to greatness was to think a few moves ahead.

Lost in thought, he hadn't noticed someone enter. Not until their shadow swallowed his. There was only one reason for anyone to be here.

Angelo did not turn to see his killer. He closed his eyes, concentrated on the heat of the water soothing his old muscles.

The rough fingers around his throat felt like ice.

Checkmate, was his last thought.

"Couldn't have happened to a nicer guy." Riley leaned forward, elbows on the table. "So our star witness is free to go. We'll honor our immunity agreement for his past sins." Riley's eyes went hard. "Not his present ones."

"That's a lot of information to process."

"I'd love to keep you for questioning, Lonagan. Rake you over the coals. But there's a lawyer out there whose shoes cost more than our lives, and he's threatening to sue the whole world if we don't kick you loose."

Riley stood and stretched his back. Lonny did the same.

"Tell Whitey to get gone and stay gone."

Lonny didn't care about any of it. He had done his job The boy was with his father. He was relieved that there would probably be no retribution now for Angelo Junior. Some people had to die. That was a price Lonny was willing to pay. He thought sadly of Vilma. He would have paid much more to save his own son, a much higher price.

His new lawyer got Lonny out quickly and gave him a ride home. The attorney's shiny black Porsche Carreira gleamed like his polished shoes.

"Mr. Scarlotti wanted to express how grateful he was to you."

"Don't mention it."

"He would also like to discuss some possible future employment with you."

Half a chuckle escaped Lonny's mouth. "Please tell Mr. Scarlotti, thanks but no thanks."

A tight smile on the lawyer's lips. "That was the answer he expected."

The drive was so smooth, Lonny almost didn't want it to end. But it did. The lawyer pulled to the curb, handed Lonny a fat envelope.

"Mr. Scarlotti wanted to make it very clear, if you are ever in need...."

Lonny smiled and stepped out of the car.

When he got to his apartment door, he heard activity inside. He reached for his pistol but it was in an evidence room downtown. Fuck it, he thought, and pushed open the door.

Kelly, his ex-wife, supervised workers as they finished replacing the glass door in his living room. She had already cleaned the floor where Kat had died.

"Hi," was all she said.

"Thank you."

"You're welcome."

"I'm sorry."

"I know you are, Dylan."

"For everything."

"I know." She hugged herself.

He grimaced as he bent and touched the cool floor; the sun made the polish shine. "I guess some messes are harder to clean up than others."

"How did it go with the police?"

"Could have gone worse."

The two repairmen were picking up their tools. "We're all set here, folks," one of them said.

They smiled at both as they packed up and left.

Kelly slid on her coat. "I guess I'll see you around town, Lonny." She opened the door and turned.

"I hope so."

"The boy is safe?"

"I hope so."

She walked away before he could see the tears in her eyes, before she could see the tears in his. Maybe that was what finally ended things between them. They had grown tired of seeing each other cry.

# 25

*If he isn't working, Lonny often finds himself at Mike's Pastries in the late afternoon, an espresso and some sort of confection in front of him. The longer he waits, the tighter the fingers of worry squeeze his heart, until finally Christopher Scarlotti strolls by, his backpack stuffed, and more often than not, a dreamy, melancholic expression on his face. Lonny knows that look well, when you can't decide whether it's better to remember or forget.*

*Usually, the boy waves at Lonny and Lonny waves back.*

*Sometimes, Christopher comes inside.*

*"Hi, Mr. Lonagan."*

*"Haven't I told you about a hundred times to call me Dylan?"*

*The boy smiles. "Yes, Mr. Lonagan."*

*Today, Christopher hands Lonny a postcard, like he'll do on occasion. Always from somewhere warm. This one is from California.*

*"How's school, Christopher?"*

*"Okay."*

*"Can I get you something? Gelato?"*

*"No thanks. I gotta head home."*

*"Say hi to your dad."*

*"Okay, Mr. Lonagan."*

*Lonny gives him a sharp look but they both laugh, then Christopher leaves.*

*The postcard has a chess move on it, and a note:*

Knight to Q6

Okay, you bastard, I'll take your queen.

Happy?

*Lonny watches Christopher disappear down the street, another knight with no queen.*

Mike Miner lives and writes in Connecticut. He is the author of *Prodigal Sons* (Full Dark City Press) and *Everything She Knows* (Solstice E-Books). His stories can be found in the anthologies *Protectors: Stories to Benefit PROTECT* and *Pulp Ink 2* as well as in places like *All Due Respect*, *Burnt Bridge*, *Narrative*, *PANK*, *The Flash Fiction Offensive*, *Shotgun Honey* and others.